DOCTOR WHO

THE WITCHFINDERS

Based on the BBC television adventure
The Witchfinders by Joy Wilkinson

JOY WILKINSON

BOOKS

BBC Books, an imprint of Ebury Publishing
20 Vauxhall Bridge Road,
London SW1V 2SA

BBC Books is part of the Penguin Random House group of companies
whose addresses can be found at global.penguinrandomhouse.com

First published by BBC Books in 2021

www.penguin.co.uk

A CIP catalogue record for this book is available from the British Library

ISBN 9781785945021

Editorial Director: Albert DePetrillo
Project Editor: Steve Cole
Cover design: Two Associates
Cover illustration: Anthony Dry
Production: Sian Pratley

Typeset in 11.4/14.6 pt Adobe Caslon Pro
by Integra Software Services Pvt. Ltd, Pondicherry

Printed and bound in Great Britain by Clays Ltd, Elcograf S.p.A.

The authorised representative in the EEA is Penguin Random House Ireland,
Morrison Chambers, 32 Nassau Street, Dublin D02 YH68.

Penguin Random House is committed to a sustainable future for
our business, our readers and our planet. This book is made
from Forest Stewardship Council® certified paper.

MIX
Paper from
responsible sources
FSC® C018179

Contents

For Dylan and Joel
with love and hope

1

Dear Doctor

There are so many reasons why I shouldn't be here, writing this. Writing anything is enough to get me killed. A girl like me, whence I came, has no business knowing how to hold a pen, let alone dare to tell her truth with it. Especially not my truth, about a place that has been obliterated from history, about the most powerful man in the world, and about a woman with even more power, who cannot possibly be proven to exist. But I know that you do exist, and you must read this and come to my rescue before the dawn light silvers the walls of this gaol, or else I shall be hanged.

2

And Justice for All

'When we get out of here, we will kill them all.'

Sselde the Morax Queen led her King and the Morax Army through the endless dark of the dungeon, a vast labyrinth specially constructed to outwit them. Its walls were impenetrable yet in constant motion, made from pitch-black magma dense with AI. It was sticky as warm creosote and made wet sounds like tongues and slugs as it shifted into new formations, not simply cutting off their path with a dead end, but creating ever more complex structures, coral-like corridors and impossible staircases, that teased Sselde into thinking that, if only she could be clever enough, the Morax still stood a chance of escaping.

That chance was the worst part of the punishment, clinging on to it even though she knew this place was tailored to confound the instincts of its prisoners, and to evolve several steps ahead of their ability to learn how it worked. So, no matter what strategy the Queen employed, she could never find the way out and make good on her blood promise. But still, the thought of massacring their captors kept her going; fuelled her resolve even in the face of certain failure.

Failure was new to the Morax. Rising from the ruins of a civilisation that nuked itself, they were precision-tooled to thrive in hostile environments. And if the planets they annexed weren't naturally tough terrain, they were soon made toxic by the Morax's methods of warfare. Bombing other races to the brink of extinction created the kind of landscape where they felt at home. Any stragglers who survived soon became sport for the Morax to pick off with their blastwaves of psychic energy, as they stalked through their new playground of rubble and flames, tall and strong and merciless.

This killer combination of Olympian build, brutal MO and cockroach constitution – insect virtues in a rangy, armoured humanoid frame – had seen the Morax undefeated for generations, and even Sselde's latest campaigns in the Tyor Quadrant were an unqualified success. It enraged her that their captivity was not the consequence of a loss. No one had beaten the Morax on the battlefield. It had been just another glorious day invading a strategic target, leading her beloved husband and elite forces through the remains of a cathedral, when Sselde heard the cry. A baby, buried under the debris. It happened sometimes, the weakest creatures survived a major catastrophe only to go and die by the more mundane matters of lack of food and air. Unless someone saved them.

Sselde stopped, bent down to locate the cry. She unfurled a long, elegant arm and picked away the heavy stone that trapped the infant. There he was, a boy as radiant as the baby on the stained-glass windows in Earth's cathedrals, and Sselde looked down at him tenderly, like Mary gazing in the manger. She still had the stone in her fist. She raised it up, and brought it down, hard –

Before the stone could split the soft skull, the baby's eyes blazed white light and it lifted its hand. The Morax dematerialised. All of them – Queen, King, Army – vanished from the cathedral and found themselves in court for contravening some ancient holy law Sselde hadn't even heard of.

'But you do know that what you did is wrong? To kill an innocent.'

Disembodied voices from outside the mirrored dome of the courtroom, all kinds of voices, but speaking as one. It could be a council of all the races they'd decimated, or it could be God embodied in a chorus of cherubic white-eyed babies, Sselde didn't care. She wanted to kill them all.

'I didn't kill it. But I would have and I wouldn't be wrong. It was my territory, my rules. The Morax does not answer to you.' Her voice bounced off the mirrored walls. Her reflection raged back at her, as the voices answered calmly, harmonious.

'You do now. Finally the Morax will answer for the deaths of all your prisoners of war, by becoming prisoners yourselves.'

'Why? I've lost no wars. I've signed no treaties. If you want your justice, you must try to beat us.'

'We do not kill, not even the guilty. Our territory is life and you must play by our rules. We sentence you to pass eternity in prison.'

The mirrors melted away, revealing the glistening black magma walls behind. The court became the dungeon and they had been here ever since, forging on through the darkness for almost a year, fury undimmed. Looking back, Sselde realised that those mirrors had been taking the data they needed to calibrate the AI; to imbue it with her cruelty, the Morax mind set. Perhaps if she'd shown regret, contrition, there would be a way out of the prison. But now she knew, it would never yield. All that kept her alive was hate, rage at the injustice, and that delectable fantasy –

'When we get out of here, we will kill them all.'

'Stop saying that or we will never get out,' the Army Captain spoke up to her for the first time. He hadn't meant to. He knew the consequences. But the words had been festering in his gut for months and, with one more prod from Sselde, they rushed up his throat and escaped. It felt good – something like freedom – until she turned on him.

Sselde went to snap his neck for insubordination. A hand held her back; the King, intrigued. 'Let him speak?'

At least he knew to ask nicely. Sselde wrested her hand away, and nodded to the Captain, who chose his words more carefully, now there was a chance to persuade her.

'What if the judgment did not end in that court?' he said. 'The walls are still learning, so they may change if we change. Our anger has been keeping us trapped. The stronger it is, the more impossible it is to escape. But if we truly repent, we could yet be released.'

'You want us to weaken?'

'No, Your Majesty. To change.'

Sselde looked from him to the King to the soldiers, all listening intently, waiting to see what she'd do. She snapped the Captain's neck, ripped out his bleeding heart and took a bite.

'The dungeon is living. It responds like all living beings. To force.'

The Army cheered. She threw them his body to feast on and turned to feed her King. 'Come, my love, taste blood and fear and never forget how powerful we are.'

Suddenly the walls shifted in a new way, splitting open. A shaft of light broke through the jagged crack. A way out. Sselde's eyes lit up, she kissed the King with her bloody lips, and turned to her Army, triumphant: 'Let us kill them all.'

They cheered louder, faith and fury restored, then left their Captain's entrails and followed her through the crack into the light. A next-level courtroom of pure light and those wretched, smug voices again, decreeing that the Morax were too unsafe even for the dungeon. By killing one of their own, Sselde had condemned them to the next level of punishment.

'It is not our place to take life, so in your case we have no choice but to break it down to its essence and subdue it to the highest degree of security for the maximum sentence. Eternity.'

The white light intensified with fierce heat and searing noise, drowning out Sselde's roar of indignation as the Morax disintegrated from its corporeal form into its core substance, to be incarcerated on a random, barren planet far away. Pure hate, locked away forever.

Almost.

3

A Celebration

Instead of incarcerating its inmates, the TARDIS set them free to explore far and wide, back and forth, through time and space.

Right now, it was hurtling on a course towards Westminster Abbey on the bright, frost-flowered morning of 15 January 1559. After their tangle with sinister robots and exploding bubble-wrap at Kerblam!, the whole fam favoured a trip into a tech-free era, far enough back to not jeopardise the existence of any close relatives, but somewhere civilised enough to have decent grub and no cesspits to mess up Ryan's new trainers. Graham suggested the coronation of Elizabeth I, as the feast and flooring were bound to be top notch, and also because his recording of Cate Blanchett's film *Elizabeth* had clashed with his series-linked *Bake Off* repeats, so it seemed easier to hop back and watch the real deal rather than hunt down a DVD.

Warping towards its destination, the TARDIS and Graham were both having a wobble. As the Doctor skittered around the console, coaxing the cranky ship back under her control, Graham shared the source of his worries:

'I know normally we don't bother, but don't you think we should dress up a bit for this? It *is* a coronation. I don't feel right rocking up in my anorak.'

'That's not an anorak, Graham, it's a sports-leisure jacket and you look gorgeous in it.' The Doctor's eyes glinted, teasing: 'Hang on, is that what you're worried about, that you might catch Liz the First's eye and change the course of history when she falls for you?'

'Nah, he just wants to wear tights and a codpiece,' Ryan grinned.

'She'd definitely fall for me then!' Graham winked, instantly turning Ryan's grin into a grimace.

'She fell for me once, good Queen Bess,' the Doctor fondly recalled. 'Wanted to marry me. Then another time she wanted to lop off my head. We've had a few tangles over the years, but I don't think she'll recognise me now. Anyhow she hasn't met me yet, technically.'

'We shouldn't meet her.' Yaz had been imagining the event beyond what outfit to wear. 'Just think, she's on the brink of becoming queen. She lost her dad, her sister, and now it's all down to her. She's going to be freaking out, trying to stay focused. Like I was, getting my police commendation. We should sit at the back and keep a low profile, not like my folks did to me, waving wildly, Dad filming on his iPad, blocking the view.'

It made Yaz blush. It made the Doctor flush with pride and want to watch the footage, or go one better. 'Aw, we should go back and see that, really freak you out.'

Yaz smiled, knew she understood, as the Doctor went on: 'This is a tricky time for women, and whatever Liz's shortcomings, no one can say that she didn't blaze a trail. So let's keep it classy, at least until the canapés. *Then* we can go crazy. Ah, there we go.' At last the ship stopped shuddering and seemed to sigh as it settled down to land. 'What was all that about, eh? Maybe the TARDIS is getting nervous too. If her chameleon circuits still worked, she'd be decked out in her best oak panelling and tapestries. Never mind, we'll blend in perfectly, like we always do. Let's go grab us a pew with a view.'

The Doctor led the way, striding out of the TARDIS ...

... into the woods. A clearing in the woods, to be precise, with a carpet of mulchy brown leaves below and a vast white wintry sky above, through the bare tree branches.

'You have got to be kidding me,' Ryan looked down at the black mud seeping up through the rotting leaves, staining his pristine soles.

'I know London was less built up back then, but surely Westminster wasn't this – um –' Graham peered around, searching for the right word – 'woody?'

The Doctor was a tad flummoxed too, until she remembered: 'St James's Park! Liz's dad Henry VIII made it into a deer park for his hunting pleasure. A luscious boggy oasis, slap bang in the heart of London.' She turned 360 degrees, getting her bearings, then apparently guessed: 'This way.'

'St James's Park?' Graham raised an eyebrow then shrugged. 'If you say so, Doc.'

They followed the flapping tails of her coat, weaving through the ghostly trees, Ryan stepping-stoning across gnarled roots and leaf piles in a futile bid to avoid the splatter.

(Behind them, unheard and unseen, there was a sickly slithering sound as a thin tendril of mud lifted up from the ground, like a dirt-encrusted finger, pointing, as if feeling which way the wind was blowing. When they had passed out of view, it melted back into the earth. Whichever way the wind was blowing, it was surely for ill.)

'I don't remember St James's Park being this big,' Graham ventured after a while.

'No, you're right,' conceded the Doctor. 'Maybe it's Hyde Park. Henry turned that into a deer park too. The big guy couldn't get enough of them.'

'You'd think there'd be more deer.' Yaz didn't need her detective skills to tell this wasn't any park and the Doctor was doing her misguided motivational thing of keeping their spirits up while she sussed out exactly how much trouble they were in.

The Doctor was indeed sussing that out, her senses on overdrive, inhaling deeply, tasting the air, scanning for distant sounds and shifts in light that could give her a clue, all under the guise of a bracing winter walk. Finally she caught something – strains of music drifting on the chill breeze. An upbeat tune, wrought by whistles and strings. So at least they were on Earth. Probably. Hurdy-gurdies were also popular on Rynskil 9, but their trees were sentient and would surely have said hello by now.

Feeling increasingly upbeat, she marched towards and in step with the tune. 'Didn't I tell you? Celebrations are kicking off already.'

They certainly were, but not quite as anticipated.

They broke through the trees to find the party was more on the scale of a small car boot sale than a coronation. There were a handful of stalls plus a couple of colourful minstrels busking while a few dozen merrymakers danced and caroused. Around them, chimneys smoked on the thatched roofs of rustic cottages, filling the air with that rich wood-smoke scent that always reminded Yaz of Hallowe'en and

Bonfire Night. She wondered if Bonfire Night existed yet, wherever – whenever – they were.

Which is when she noticed that, despite the apparent jollity, the revellers were wearing masks that were more fitting for a home-invasion in a horror film than fun festivities. Sharp pointed noses, exaggerated sad faces, or icy blank expressions flashed by as they danced. Yaz felt unsettled by the contrast, but reminded herself that some of her trick or treating outfits had a pretty freaky mix, not least the combo of silver sari, vampire mask and plastic truncheon she'd thrown together when Izzy Flint had invited her out last minute with the cool kids and she'd panicked and had to raid her old dressing up box … only to find it was a wind-up and they'd tricked her, running away screaming whenever she got near. The trick was on Yaz, and she hadn't needed an outfit after all. It seemed she was horrific enough to some people just in her own skin.

The masks and the smoke scent transported her back into that moment faster than a TARDIS – the shame swelling, raw in her throat – and she felt small and lost again, even though now she was surrounded by true friends who would never trick her. They chattered away inanely with no idea of her painful memories. Yaz tuned back into them, grateful.

'Admit it, Doc,' said Graham, 'this is *not* the coronation of Elizabeth I.'

'It's not front row seats, Graham, I'll give you that, but history's always better when you get down and dirty, see how life really was.' The Doctor was sniffing again, eyes darting around, calibrating just how wide of the mark they'd materialised.

'Looks like a street party,' Ryan said. 'Ye olde hipster pop-up happening.'

'So where are we?' Graham pushed.

'The TARDIS is being a bit stubborn at exact readings,' was all the Doctor would admit. Then something caught her eye, distracting her, and she dashed off: 'Apple bobbing! I love apple bobbing!'

A scruffy urchin stood behind a huge barrel brimming with rainwater and rosy apples. He beamed as the mad lady sprinted over and plunged her head in deep, demonstrating a well-honed technique for nabbing the best prize in minimal time.

While the Doctor was submerged, Yaz shared her suspicions: 'It looks more like Hallowe'en, don't you think?'

The Doctor emerged, dripping, with an apple clamped between her teeth. She had either heard Yaz or had the same thought, because the moment her mouth was fruit-free, she asked: 'What day is this?'

'Sunday. We do this every week,' the boy sniffed, cheerfully matter-of-fact.

That seemed weird to Yaz, but she supposed farmer's markets were every Sunday too. The Doctor seemed delighted, declaring, 'Happy Sunday!' as she took a bite.

Graham leaned into Yaz, shared a clue he'd picked up on: 'Northern accent, we must be close to home.'

Before Yaz could respond, there was a loud CLANG!

Suddenly the party stopped and everyone stood still and silent.

An old man with a long white beard was ringing a hand-bell, a bit like Father Christmas turning up at the end of an infants' school disco to hand out pressies, but with no pressies and a much more ominous tone as he announced: 'Mistress Savage demands your presence. The ceremony will begin.'

The boy left the apple-bobbing barrel and went to join the rest of the revellers, who had stopped revelling and were walking away from the village in a sombre procession. The drumbeat started up again, slow and steady, definitely not for dancing to. For walking, and for beating out time, like a steady, dread-filled countdown.

'Anyone else missing the party vibe all of a sudden?' Graham asked, unnerved.

'Come on,' the Doctor set off, intrigued, following the crowd out of the village.

The last to leave was a man dressed in black from hat to riding boots, with black leather gloves and a long black cape. He had been sitting on a wall beside an ugly turnip jack-o'-lantern, watching through the narrow slits of his plague mask. The mask had a long spiked beak that doctors used to protect themselves from airborne miasmas. Through the slits, the man's eyes lit up like the jack-o'-lantern's, aflame with excitement. He stalked after the procession, into the woods.

4

In the Water

'Where are they all going?' Yaz wondered as they followed the procession down a track through thicker woodland, keeping step with the drum. There was a sense of tension, excited anticipation.

The Doctor munched on her apple, musing. She knew that the TARDIS, for reasons of its own, had landed them somewhere and some time other than intended, though she was still struggling to pin down anything more specific than Northern England on a Sunday, possibly in the early modern period. But wherever and whenever it was, there were rules to be followed, so she issued an urgent reminder designed to avoid any more Rosa Parks or Punjab-style timeline problems cropping up.

'Whatever this is, I need you all to remember. The important thing about our dips into the past – do not interfere with the fundamental fabric of history.'

'Even if something's not right?' Yaz asked. It certainly felt that way. She could almost imagine that someone was watching them.

Just then she was distracted by the sound of sobbing up ahead. Yaz caught up with a girl in a grey cape, saw her tear-streaked face hidden in the hood. 'Are you OK?' she asked. 'Can you tell us what's going on here?'

The girl looked at her, patently not OK and more unnerved than comforted by Yaz's concern. The girl dipped her head and hurried away, through the crowd.

The Doctor spat out her mouthful and gagged. The core of the apple was rotten brown and home to a fat twitching maggot.

Ryan took the apple from her and flung it hard, deep into the woods.

(It landed with a splat in a murky patch of dirt … where, unseen, another mud tendril slithered up from the earth, seeking. The tendril reached out to feel the apple core, ran its grimy tip over the maggot, briefly interested, and then rejected it. The tendril shrivelled back down and vanished.)

The Doctor was pretty sure there was something rotten here, beyond the dodgy apple. She shuddered and walked on to the drumbeat, out to where the skeleton trees thinned and a wide, rushing river cut through the land.

That's when Graham saw it. Looming across the horizon, a huge, dark hump of earth, shrugging off the weak winter sunlight. Ryan, Yaz and even the Doctor felt a chill as they saw it, knowing in their bones that it was something uncanny. But Graham knew exactly what it was. He had been here before – or was going to be here, centuries from now.

'Guys, that's Pendle Hill,' he said. 'We're in Lancashire.'

Even though they had never been here, the others had heard of Pendle, in history classes or TARDIS files, misty memories from which one chilling word emerged: *witches*.

Suddenly it all made sense, as they took in the crowd at the riverbank and saw the sight that everyone's eyes were glued to.

An old woman was suspended out over the water, chained to a wooden chair made from the twisted branches of a felled tree. Its mighty trunk stretched out from the bank, forming the arm of a jarringly beautiful yet utterly evil contraption with a lever at its base manned by a mean-faced guard. A ducking stool, designed to test whether the old woman was a witch or not. That was the stated purpose of the stool, but it proved way more effective at inflicting torture, instilling fear and providing lurid entertainment for the waiting crowd of onlookers.

But not all of them were looking forward to this.

Willa Twiston, her tears hidden by the cape hood tight about her face, pushed her way to the edge of the riverbank – as close as she dared get to the guard whose sword glinted sharp and whose ears pricked up to catch any incriminating evidence. She knew the words pounding through her mind could be taken as a spell and was straining not to speak them aloud, but when her eyes met her granny's she couldn't help herself.

Her granny was the woman lashed to the stool; not a witch, but a wise woman who had raised Willa from childhood and now desperately needed her to cope alone.

Mother Twiston saw her granddaughter and murmured to her: 'Hush, Willa, don't cry. I will still be with you, in the water, in the fire, in the air, in the earth.'

It was a prayer, a poem, but Willa wished it had the power of a spell, that it felt stronger. She chimed in under her breath, echoing her granny, letting her know – neither of them would ever really be alone. 'I will still be with you, in the water, in the fire, in the air, in the earth.'

For a moment they felt connected, almost comforted, but were cut asunder again as the bell rang again, bringing everyone to attention, and focusing that attention on another woman in a scarlet dress and a black hat with a grand white feather, standing on a wooden platform, grimly surveying her people. This was Becka Savage, a small, striking, tough woman, who could sometimes be brutal, just like this land she owned.

She took in her audience, making them wait before gracing them with her words, and then announced: 'People of Bilehurst Cragg, we are forced to meet here once again. Satan stalks this land. We must continue to root him out and do whatever it takes to save the soul of our village. Let us put the accused to the test.'

The Doctor listened in horror as exactly where and when they had landed sank in. She whispered rapidly, filling the others in: 'This is a witch trial. Early seventeenth century. If memory serves, there were two spates in Lancashire, 1612 and 1634. My guess is this looks like the first. But it shouldn't be happening here. The so-called witches were tried and hanged in Lancaster, at the castle. So this is … something else.'

She looked upstream, where a stone bridge crossed the river, and surveyed the set-up at the other side, where the guards stood between the ducking stool and the woman on the platform. The Doctor guessed this must be the 'Mistress Savage' who had demanded their presence and seemed to be in charge of proceedings. Even if the Doctor could get over there in time, could she stop them? Should she?

Mistress Savage went on: 'Mother Twiston, you stand accused of witchcraft, and shall be tried by my ducking stool, hewn from the mightiest tree on Pendle Hill. If you drown, you are innocent. If you survive, you are a witch and shall be hanged!'

'So either way she dies?' Ryan said. 'This is way too dark for me.'

Not for the rest of the crowd, which was getting rowdy, impatient.

'We've got to do something, Doctor,' said Yaz.

'Ah, the Doc said don't interfere. You said don't interfere, right?' Graham checked.

The Doctor stayed laser-focused on Mother Twiston. She could almost feel the terror coursing through the old woman and the Herculean bravery that held it down.

Mistress Savage gave the signal: 'Duck the witch!'

The crowd cheered and chanted: 'Duck the witch! Duck the witch!'

The guard released the lever. Mother Twiston closed her eyes, but felt the terror finally take over as the stool plummeted down and hit the water. SPLASH!

'Granny!' someone cried out, anguished. The girl in the cape. So that's why she was crying. Because this woman was ducking her poor, defenceless grandmother.

That did it. The Doctor couldn't hold her urge back any longer. She pulled off her coat and shoved it at Ryan.

'Meet me on the other side,' she said, and ran to the riverbank.

SPLASH!

The Doctor dived in, hearts almost stopping in shock at the freezing water, but pummelling on, summoning the strength she needed to swim against the slamming current. The crowd's chant died as they found something even more thrilling to watch than a witch ducking – a small woman with a shock of blonde hair, cutting through the icy water with swift, powerful strokes, out to where the ducking stool was submerged. She heaved in a last breath and dove down, down, vanishing beneath the swirling water.

'So much for not interfering,' said Ryan.

Yaz pushed past him and Graham to lead the way. 'Over the bridge, come on.'

They ran fast through the rubbernecking crowd, past the crying girl in the cape, who stood rooted to spot as she watched a blonde woman pulling Mother Twiston's body through the water towards the far riverbank.

'Who dares interfere with this trial?' Mistress Savage was ranting. 'Thirty-five witches we have tried and still Satan surrounds us. We shall not be stopped. You will be punished for your interference. The trials are sacred. They are the will of God!'

'I've got you, it's all right,' the Doctor gasped as she pulled the old woman out. She couldn't feel her fingers, her limbs, but they knew what to do, defaulting to their almost involuntary impulse to save any helpless creature from an unjust fate. She heaved hard and staggered backwards until they were both safely on the muddy shore, just as Yaz, Ryan and Graham pelted down the slope to help.

But by then, even her numb fingers had begun to sense what the Doctor dreaded most of all: she had failed. Yaz skidded to her knees in the mud by the body and soon confirmed it with a regret-heavy nod.

Mother Twiston was just a body now. All life sucked out by the pitiless river. The double-punchbag hearts in the Doctor's chest might have been able to keep hammering, but a single, well-worn human heart had no chance of coping, however warm and loving it had been, however fiercely it had fought.

'Is she alive?' her granddaughter called out from across the water, where hope still glimmered. It died as she saw the looks on their faces.

'I'm sorry,' the Doctor called back, even more gutted as the girl's face crumpled, devastated.

Mistress Savage strode over from the platform, face twisted in fury.

'Now we have no way of knowing if Mother Twiston was a witch or not,' she fumed. 'Guards, whip these wanderers off this bank and then seize Willa Twiston. We can take no chances.'

The guards pulled their swords. The Doctor didn't flinch. Seeing this tyrant turn her sights on the grieving girl across the river, the Doctor's blood was boiling. No matter that she was freezing, soaking wet, and had a sword-point in her face, she gave Mistress Savage a blast from both barrels: 'Leave her alone! I'd bet my life neither of these women were witches, but you, Mistress Savage, are without question, a murderer.'

The woman bristled. 'Who are you to address me this way?' The Doctor could tell she was affronted but still smart enough to check who she was about to run through just in case they were important.

'I'll tell you who I am.' The Doctor stood tall, reached for her psychic paper … and realised it was in the pocket of her coat, which was still with Ryan. 'Sorry, one sec.' She scampered back to root through the pockets and find it, then came back, totally styling it out, brandishing the psychic paper with gusto and hoping for the best.

Mistress Savage read it and stared in confusion. 'Witchfinder General?'

The Doctor checked the paper and grinned, ready to work it to her advantage. The ways of the paper were mysterious, but sometimes it played a blinder.

'That's right, Witchfinder General, with my crack team, taking over this village. Right, gang?'

At her glance, the gang owned it, standing together like a force to be reckoned with. Ryan and Yaz grew stern and serious, while Graham glowered at Becka, reaching for the right turn of phrase: 'Yeah, because *you* are in special measures.'

Not massively seventeenth century, but he sold it well. The Doctor approved.

'Now do you recognise our authority?' she challenged, putting pressure on the figurehead in front of the villagers, who watched, hooked, as the drama unfolded.

The guards sheathed their blades. Mistress Savage bowed her head. 'I do beg your pardon, Mistress Witchfinder. Please come to my home, we must talk in private.'

'If you swear not to hurt that girl or anyone else.'

'If that is your wish, you have the command.'

The Doctor took charge, shouted her commands across the river. 'Everybody go home. This trial is over.'

The crowd obeyed their new mistress and moved off, not even daring to gossip about what had gone down until they were safely out of earshot, back in their homes. Only the girl in the cape stayed behind, fresh tears budding up as a new task loomed.

'I have to bury her,' she called out, timid, as if she might get in trouble for it

The Doctor nodded, reassuring, and bent down to close Mother Twiston's eyes. The eyelashes were still damp and river water streaked the old woman's face like tears. The Doctor brushed them away, gently, intent on righting this wrong and fixing whatever was rotten at the core of Bilehurst Cragg.

In the trees, the man in black had watched everything, his breath hot and heavy inside the stifling mask. He snapped a stick between his black-gloved hands and decided – he couldn't stand back and watch a moment longer. Now was the time to act.

5

Enter the King

Squelching across a dank field that was more mud than grass, Ryan stopped worrying about his trainers. The stakes were life and death now, and the Doctor had risked everything to try to save Mother Twiston. He looked at Yaz and Graham marching alongside him, keeping quiet for now. But Ryan knew they had to own their new roles and take charge of this hunt – not for witches, but for what was really going on.

At least this Savage woman was still deferring to the Doctor. 'Please forgive me, mistress,' she bowed her head again, angelic white feather fluttering. 'If I'd have known who you were, I'd have bowed to your authority immediately.'

The Doctor fixed Becka with a steely glare: 'So tell me who are you exactly, and what gives you authority here?'

'I am Becka Savage, landowner of Bilehurst Cragg.' Her deference flickered, showing a glimpse of the arrogant leader again, but she quickly hid it and added a layer of grieving widow for good measure. 'It belonged to my late husband and passed to me when he died. I have tried to be a benevolent leader, but it's very difficult in these times, especially for a woman.'

She looked at the Doctor, as if hopeful for a kindred spirit, a sisterhood to help share the stresses of witchfinding, but the Doctor cut that dead and instead looked around at the fields. All were empty except for the naked trees and muddy puddles.

'If you're the landowner, why are you walking? Where are all the horses?'

'Horses are banned in Bilehurst. They are creatures of Satan. I had them all shot.'

Ryan gaped at Becka in disbelief. Deference, grieving widow and kindred spirit had all withered away to reveal the madness beneath. The messed-up mind of a woman whose worldview had warped beyond human understanding. He watched her speed up, pacing ahead of the Doctor, as if there was nothing more to be said on the matter.

He turned to Yaz. 'How'd you get through to someone like that?'

Graham cut in with his own troubles, which had galloped way beyond anoraks. 'Here, Doc, I've done the old Pendle Witches walking trail. Nobody ever mentioned Bilehurst Cragg. Never heard of it. And surely it'd be infamous if she's gone and killed thirty-five people.'

'Thirty-six now,' Ryan reminded him. 'Maybe she wipes this place off the map?'

If that was the truth, the Doctor looked ready to change it. 'We're gonna find out what happened,' she said. 'And how we can make Becka Savage stop.'

Rearing up at the top of the slope was a huge manor house, dark-bricked and brooding. The Doctor surveyed it: Savage Hall should have looked much more alluring, given that it would at least be warmer inside, but, like its owner, it was distinctly unwelcoming. 'That looks like a place we'll find some answers.'

Yaz was glancing back towards the village in the distance, her investigative instincts tugging at her sleeve. 'It's not the only place, though, Doctor. Police make this mistake all the time, getting caught up with the perpetrators, sidelining the victims. I want to go and find that girl who just lost her gran. Willa Twiston.'

How was it that Yaz Khan could warm the Doctor's cockles even when she was borderline hypothermic? Yaz's capacity to give a monkey's about the forgotten in all corners of the universe blazed hotter than any hearth in Savage Hall. The Doctor nodded and laid out the plan: 'We'll deal with her ladyship, while you go and do some family liaison. We'll meet you in a bit. Hopefully by then I'll have dried off!'

The Doctor grinned, sending a shot of warmth back to Yaz as she headed off on her solo mission. Then she turned and led Ryan and Graham after Becka to Savage Hall, determined to get to the bottom of it all.

Soon the Doctor's clothes had gone from dripping wet to merely damp as she crouched in front of a fireplace in the grand wood-panelled room that Becka kept for best. Graham perched on the beautifully upholstered window seat and watched as the Doctor toasted her fingers and Becka bustled around on best behaviour. By Graham's reckoning, she'd been a good hostess so far, ushering them in here, ordering maids to fetch refreshments and stoke the fire. Now she was pouring wine and trying to make this into some kind of social occasion, as if her own character and motives weren't on trial.

Ryan declined a goblet, hands in his pockets, strong and silent. Graham was tempted to have a drop, but thought he'd better not and reclined in the window seat, trying to temper his excitement at chilling out in this stately home with the memory of that poor old woman hitting the water. This wasn't a museum trip, this was living history and that woman was dead. They couldn't let Becka get away with it, however much she sucked up. *She can shove her claret where the sun don't shine!* he thought.

'I hope the fire has warmed you,' Becka toadied over to the Doctor. 'Some wine?'

'Nope.' The Doctor was having none of this sham hospitality and cracked on with the grilling. 'So your witch trials have become a weekly event with a village celebration?'

Becka nodded, all innocence: 'Any moment where a witch is uncovered and Satan driven out has to be a cause for celebration. We will not stop until that work is done.'

'You keep saying Satan, but how is Satan manifesting himself here?'

'Blighting the crops, bewitching animals, plaguing people with fits, sickness, visions.'

Ryan struggled to follow: 'If all that's Satan, where do the witches come into it?'

Becka stared at him, as if the answer was obvious. 'They are in league with him. Kill the witches, defeat Satan. As King James has written in his new Bible, thou shalt not suffer a witch to live.'

'Ah, yes, but it also says love thy neighbour,' the Doctor beamed, 'which is why we've come, to help you fix your problems without killing anyone. It's what King James would want.'

Becka took the hit, it looked for a moment like she might be willing to go with it, but just then –

The heavy door swung wide and a man in black burst in.

Graham stood up. Ryan tensed. The Doctor braced, ready for battle.

The man whipped away his cloak and hat and tossed them to a waiting maid who seemed slightly stunned but unharmed. Then he moved into the room and peeled off the mask with a dramatic flourish, revealing the red-bearded face of a middle-aged man, who Becka recognised in a quickening heartbeat.

'King James!' She sank to the floor in a fathom-deep curtsey. No need to feign any deference with this man. Her awe was palpable.

The others gave a quick bow, gazing at each other, caught completely off-guard.

James was still caught up with his entrance speech, delivered in a lusty Scottish burr. 'You may prostrate yourselves before me, God's chosen ruler and Satan's greatest foe, come to vanquish the scourge of witchcraft across the land!'

King James enjoyed the silence, letting it sink in, before adding, 'Forgive the mask, I have enemies everywhere and have to travel incognito. Also, I rather like the drama.'

He spoke aside, with a chuckle, taking them into his confidence. Becka laughed too hard, nerves jangling as the King came closer, curious to inspect the strangers.

'What a peculiar ragbag of folks. And those garments – are you actors?' James rather hoped so. A huge fan of all things theatrical, James was great mates with Shakespeare and had rebranded his acting troupe the King's Men, elevating them with this highest of honours. Whereas this lowly group before him bizarrely included a woman, but perhaps she just took care of their costumes, meals and other basic needs.

'I'm the Doctor,' she said. 'We're your witchfinders, sire, as we explained to Mistress Savage.'

James peered at the official document she held out. He was less familiar with his witchfinding staff than his acting company, who tended to be less uptight, more fun, and much more aesthetically pleasing.

'Witchfinder's Assistant?' he read, appraising the Doctor with fresh scepticism.

The Doctor frowned at the paper, as James dismissed her and instead approached the elder gent, with all the warmth and bonhomie of an old comrade. 'So, you must be the Witchfinder General … ?'

'What?' the Doctor spluttered. The psychic paper had gone method, not just donning calligraphy and a parchment wash, but channelling the seventeenth century prejudices that James beamed out. For the first time she was confronted with the brick wallher new body could smash into, blocking her out of power, making her invisible, inaudible. 'Assistant?'

No one answered her. The only acknowledgement was Becka's – 'Er, she said *she* was the Witchfinder General …' – diminishing the Doctor still more before the King, making out she was lying.

But James didn't even pick up on that subterfuge. He was much too tickled, guffawing at the great wheeze: 'A woman could never be the General!'

Pure humiliation. The Doctor was itching to take James to task, but she made herself hold back, figuring out there must be some pros as well as cons to this female form in certain times on Earth. Underestimation could have its benefits. 'Silly me, I must have got all confused, mustn't I, boss?'

She fixed Graham with a look, challenging him to find a way of playing this without winding her up, while still passing muster with the King.

'Er, yeah, that's me, sire. North-West Division, promoted from Essex.'

Now James nodded, apparently finding Graham's authority convincing whatever he said. 'And these are your underlings?'

The Doctor's apoplexy flared. Ryan gave a mean dead-eye. Graham scrambled: 'It's a very flat team structure. We each have our area of expertise.'

'Even the wee lassie?' James cocked a brow at the Doctor, who'd had enough.

'Even me! Very handy undercover – set a woman to catch a woman.'

'A cunning ruse, using your innate aptitude for nosiness and gossip.'

The Doctor longed to show her aptitude for decking him, but her innate pacifism and sense of self-preservation prevailed, just. Luckily James moved on to Ryan, with a gleam in his eye.

'And what is your field of expertise, my Nubian prince – torture?' The King gave a little shudder of pleasure at the notion.

Ryan looked to Graham, lost for words, but Graham was enjoying the spectacle and had no intention of helping him out. Ryan dredged up: 'Paperwork mostly, Your Majesty.'

'Paper? How fascinating! We should talk,' James gave him a long lingering look, and then snapped into business mode, turning to Becka. 'But first, madam, word has reached me of your battle against Satan, your crusade against witchcraft, but what I saw today convinced me – you need assistance.'

'That's what we've just been saying!' the Doctor cut in.

'Hold your tongue, lassie!' James rasped. 'You stick to snooping and leave the strategy to your King. This is no time for the weak. Satan preys on the innocent even while they sleep.' His eyes locked on Becka's, which were dancing with the flames from her hellfire. 'Together, we must purify your land. Starting with the grandchild of the witch you tried today.'

A chill shot through the room. The witchfinders' silence seemed to irk James. 'A fine plan, is it not?'

The Doctor was ready to stop holding her tongue. To tell James exactly what she thought of his plan. But before she could speak, Becka stepped forward, pushing the Doctor aside and toasting the king with her goblet, gazing like he was the answer to her prayers.

'A genius plan, Your Majesty,' Becka beamed. 'Together we shall save the souls of my people from Satan – even if it means killing them all.'

6

In the Earth

Willa Twiston pulled a wooden cart that carried the carefully shrouded body of her beloved granny through the trees, into the Witches' Graveyard. Once an oasis of peace in the heart of the woods, this remote glade was now filled with uneven mounds of earth, rough crosses of wood and rocks, and sorrow hanging heavy with the mist.

The children of Bilehurst were too scared to set foot here, but it just made Willa unbearably sad, and never more so than now. She forced herself on, telling herself that Granny wouldn't mind being buried here. The ground may not be consecrated, but it was closer to the nature she had worshipped than that poor carved man on the cross in the church. Worshipping trees more than Jesus didn't make Mother Twiston a witch, and the other women buried here weren't witches either. Not even Annie Clay, the woman who started it all, and the first body who had lain on this cart, brought here by Willa and her granny, to be buried in the woods she loved, alone.

Or so they'd thought.

Annie Clay had certainly lived like a witch, deep in the woods, in a tumbledown hut shared with pigs and rats and spiders. One of her eyes was pure bloodshot white, her teeth were grey stumps, and things moved in her hair. She was older than anyone could remember, and no one knew who her family was. People said she was so ugly her parents left her in the woods to die, and better it would have been for everyone including Annie if she had. Because instead, so they said, it was the Devil who had kept her alive all these years, in exchange for her soul.

When Willa was little, she wasn't sure Annie Clay was even real. The old witch was just given as a reason to not go too deep into the woods or a reason to stay inside after dark, an excuse for why things went missing or got broken, or a threat to make Willa brush her hair and wash her face and be a good girl so as not to end up like ugly old Annie Clay. Willa didn't live with her granny back then and her mum and dad were much more God-fearing and superstitious. Perhaps something in them knew that they wouldn't live long and had to ensure a safe passage to the afterlife. So they raised their little girl to follow the rules, to believe in witches, and stay well away from the likes of Annie Clay.

Little Willa did as she was told and never crossed paths with the so-called witch, but her parents weren't so fortunate. One night on his way home from a long trip to the cattle market in Slack, her dad took a wrong turn, got lost in the woods, and found himself by Annie Clay's hut. According to his story, Annie tried to lure him inside, and when he declined and asked for help to get home, she cursed him. Foul words in an unearthly tongue that put the mark of death on him. He finally arrived home at dawn, pale and raving, on the brink of collapse. He died the next day and Willa's mother soon joined him, along with half of the village. And along with half of Slack too, if truth be told, for that was where the sickness spread from, with Annie Clay a mere detour on the way. Or maybe more than a detour, because, truth be told, men often went to that hut after dark, reassured that their women and children would never know, and would never believe that a woman as ugly as Annie Clay could be good company in her way.

That truth was never told, and Annie Clay's curse was known as the cause for the beginning of the blight on Bilehurst Cragg, which had made little orphan Willa move in with her granny, and her cousin Becka. Becka wanted Annie hanged for witchcraft there and then, but Granny cautioned tolerance, and the local landowner and justice of the peace, Richard Savage, had no appetite for witch-hunts. He was a portly widower with no offspring and only his servants and dogs to keep him company in that big house, hence he was not averse to a moonlight trip to the hut in the woods himself from time to time.

So Richard spared Annie Clay from the noose and 'the old witch got away with it,' Becka said, promising little Willa that justice would be done one day. And in many stories, little Willa would swear vengeance herself, because she loved and missed her mum and dad so much it was sometimes hard to breathe, but however they'd brought her up and whatever rules she'd learned and followed, in her heart Willa shared her granny's gift for tolerance and she did not believe in witches. Justice to her would be to find a way to heal the sickness so it never happened again. She said as much to Becka, who laughed bitterly, and said little Willa had a lot to learn.

Becka tried to teach Willa, to show how the world really worked: first by using her wiles to marry Richard Savage and then, when she still couldn't make him deliver justice, by taking over the reins when he died. Somewhere along the way, it stopped being about Willa and her parents, because Becka no longer called by or cared to associate with her family. She no longer acted like a cousin to Willa. Instead, Willa watched from afar as Becka capitalised on the darkening mood of her people to push the benefits of stability, continuity and the promise of a return to happier times, skilfully rebranding herself as their figurehead, the rightful queen of Bilehurst Cragg.

Harking back to the glory days of Queen Elizabeth, Becka pledged her fidelity to Bilehurst, refusing to remarry and casting herself as clean of soul and pure of heart, poring over the bible and dedicating herself to rooting the Devil out of their land. With seemingly no care for anything other than the fortunes of her people, Becka promised to be their lucky charm, a light to lead them through the shadowy times ahead, like the autumn sun casting its heavenly golden rays down on the demonic hill.

That's how Becka had put it, but Willa had never seen the hill as demonic. She loved it. She'd climbed up it with her granny every Sunday to tend to the ancient tree at its peak, until Becka cut it down to make her ducking stool.

Then the witch-hunts had begun.

The first woman on trial was Annie Clay, who drowned. Not a witch after all, but Becka wouldn't let her be buried in the churchyard, so Mother Twiston got Willa to fetch the wooden cart and together they brought her body here.

It wasn't the Witches' Graveyard then. It was still a peaceful glade where Granny felt that Annie's tormented soul might rest. As they dug the grave, Mother Twiston assured Willa there was no such thing as witches and that Annie had lived a sad life and found solace in the seasons, in the trees, in the wind. They said a nature prayer together, over Annie's grave, and Willa was glad that it was all over now. Granny worried it was just the start, saying she knew how people were, turning on each other out of fear and hate and feeding the witch-hunting frenzy. And so Willa learned that Granny was right. The witch-hunts went on and on and on, filling this glade up with graves, and now Granny was in one, and Willa was left alone.

She looked around at the grave markers. There were only a dozen or so. Some of the accused had floated and been hanged or burnt, or hanged and burnt, so those ashes had blown off to better places. Willa wished them well and wished that she could leave Bilehurst before she too turned to ashes. She was risking her life even being here. She had to be quick, bury her Granny and go home, or else Becka would come after her next and no one left behind would care to bury Willa. Her body would be left for the crows.

She picked up the wreath of winterberries that she had woven with Granny by the fire only last week. Even in these dark times, they held fast to faint hope that each ducking would be the last and by the solstice, they would feast and look forward to a new start. Willa struggled to cling on to that hope now, to believe in regeneration and goodness and that her Granny was still with her, when she'd never felt so utterly alone in the world. Her broken heart was barely in it, but she went through the motions for Granny's sake, plucking the blood-red berries and scattering them into the grave, saying the prayer, the spell, the words that had comforted Granny despite being powerless.

'I will still be with you, in the water, in the fire, in the air, in the earth.'

(As Willa focused on her ritual, by her boot, a large mud tendril, jagged-tipped and ridged like a spine, rose up from the mound of earth by the grave. It trembled in the air for a moment, as if tasting it, and then sharpened, sought out her bare skin where her skirts hitched up to dig. It grew fast, shook off loose dirt to reveal a muscular core of mud, a thick tentacle coming for her leg.)

'Willa, watch out!'

Willa turned to see the dark-haired girl from the riverbank bounding across the glade towards her, leaping over piles of logs. The girl looked like she was on the attack, but then why would she say watch out? Watch out for what? Willa turned back and saw –

The mud tendril, huge now, as if a giant underground mud octopus was breaking out and lashing at her. Willa froze in terror. The girl leapt past her and grabbed the spade.

'Get away from her!' The girl smashed at the tendril. It dodged, thrust back, so she twisted the spade on its side and sliced, cutting the thrashing beast off at the root. The tendril shattered, spattered her with mud. Its body disintegrated into droplets that melted away, leaving the ground as still as the grave.

'Are you all right?' the girl panted, checking on Willa.

Willa shook her head; would she ever be all right again? 'What was that?'

'I don't know what it was. But I want to help.'

Willa had coped with witch-hunts, with her granny going on trial, and drowning, but she couldn't cope with this. This undid everything that had held her together – her innate belief that witchcraft wasn't real. That Becka was wrong and God was in nature like Granny said, and there was no such thing as the Devil. But how did that explain what just happened? Suddenly Willa was overwhelmed.

'You can't help. Nobody can.'

She ran.

'Wait! Willa?' The girl called after her, but Willa was too fast, running for her life. Because now she knew – the Devil was in Bilehurst Cragg and it was coming after her.

7

Find the Witch

'I will still be with you …' I stop writing for a moment to say those words aloud again – only a whisper in case the guard hears and thinks I'm summoning Satan to help me escape. But I'm not calling out to Satan or God or even my granny. I'm calling to Yaz, Ryan, Graham and the Doctor. To that blue box that brought them to Bilehurst Cragg because it knew something, heard something, felt something shifting in the universe that meant they knew they were needed. If that happened once, it must be possible that it could happen again. That they are keeping an eye on me and will know I'm in trouble and need their help.

I've already tried writing to the King – a rather different version of events, still the truth but not the whole truth as no doubt he must be touchy about his father. I don't know if it reached Charles, no pardon has been forthcoming, and I suspect that even mentioning Bilehurst Cragg could have made things worse, sealed my fate. That must be why they brought forward the date of my execution. Before, I could at least have languished here for years, but now the King wants me dead and silenced for good. My only hope is the Doctor.

I look out through the bars at a sliver of starlight. Is she out there? Can she hear me? And feel these words as they pour from inside me into ink, onto paper, a spell of their own, becoming part of the world, part of everything that binds us together. Music on the wind for her to follow and find me. Save me. The starlight is fading, my time is running out. Please, Doctor, come and find this witch? Before it's too late.

8

Dæmonologie

The Doctor bounded up the great staircase of Savage Hall, looking for a place to debrief. Graham and Ryan followed, checking that no one was following them. The paranoia rife in Bilehurst Cragg was getting under their skin.

Once safely upstairs, the Doctor erupted: 'Becka wasn't kidding. These are hard times for women. If we're not being drowned, we're being patronised to death!' She stuck her head around a door. 'In here, quick.'

The bedroom clearly belonged to the lady of the house. A four-poster bed hung with rich fabrics and the bedside reading included a well-thumbed copy of King James's must-have manual for occult investigators, *Dæmonologie*, and a mass of biblical pamphlets filled with creepy woodcut illustrations of witches and devils. The Doctor flipped through them, searching for clues that could help make sense of the fervour.

'We are gonna help this place right, Doc? Otherwise it won't exist by the morning,' Graham worried. 'Not now those two have hit it off. I dunno which one's more barking.'

The Doctor moved on to counting through a pile of white handkerchiefs embroidered with a burgundy B. 'A dozen hankies – that's a lot.'

'Maybe she cries herself to sleep?' Ryan mused.

'Don't worry, Graham,' the Doctor answered belatedly, mind pinging in several directions at once. 'We're staying here and sorting it, even if I am just a woman.'

She went through a curtain into Becka's dressing room.

Graham hung back, as if he was back with Grace, loitering outside the fitting rooms at M&S. He shouted after her. 'Well, to be fair to King James, you are snooping.'

'I'm investigating!' The indignant Doctor took the cork from a curious glass bottle. It was empty but the scent was intriguing, like something from an apothecary. She tried to place it, but was distracted by Ryan pointing out she'd missed something, under the bed. She went back through to see him pulling out a massive axe. Now that was interesting.

'This Becka's seriously paranoid, man.' Ryan swung around fast as the door opened, blade ready for an attack.

It was only Yaz, reporting back.

'I found that girl Willa at her granny's grave doing some kind of ritual. And the next thing I know, this big kind of mud tendril thing attacked her.'

The Doctor parked all musings on scents and axes and switched to: 'Mud tendril?' She felt a tingle of anticipation. Tendrils were way more tangible than the clouds of hate and fear fuelling witch-hunts. Tendrils you could quantify, cross-reference across taxonomies of alien organisms. This was the kind of breakthrough that got her hearts racing as Yaz attempted to explain.

'Coming up out of the ground. I had to smash it to pieces. I've got it all over me.'

The Doctor pulled out her sonic and scanned the spatters across the muddy jeans, questions pouring out faster than Yaz could answer. 'Just the one mud tendril? How big? And when you say ritual, do you mean like a spell? Like she conjured it up?'

'She was scared of it. Whatever it was, it wasn't friendly.'

The Doctor checked the sonic readings, perplexed. 'Seems to be good old-fashioned Lancashire mud.' But it had got her mind whirring. This was now a battle on several fronts, not just reining in King James and Becka, but digging into mud tendrils and going to help a scared, grieving girl.

'Here's the plan – Yaz and me need to check out that mud and talk to Willa. And you two,' she turned to Graham and Ryan, who was still rocking the axe, 'stick with Becka and King James, keep them here. Make sure they don't kill anyone else.'

'King James?' Yaz frowned, wondering what she'd missed?

'It's a long story. I'll explain on the way.' The Doctor bundled her out, calling to the boys, emphatic. 'Remember – no more witch-hunts!'

In their absence, James had sent to the tavern at Barley for his precious chest of witchfinding paraphernalia, lovingly delivered by a strapping Mediterranean manservant with a black goatee beard in the style of his master. On their incognito trips, the manservant was sometimes required to play the brother or son of James, who would delight in donning a variety of disguises from blind beggar to knight errant, anything with a hood, helmet or mask that gave him access to thrilling adventures amongst his subjects with the safety of anonymity, knowing that his capable companion could step in to defend him at any time, or simply to decapitate anyone who happened to speak ill of the King.

'This is Alfonso, my personal guardian. He guards my witchfinding tools with his life.' James quivered as the young man carefully set down the heavy chest and unlocked it, revealing a cornucopia of jars, trinkets and apparatuses within.

Graham and Ryan exchanged a look, sensing this was the perfect way to play for time, indulging the King in his passions.

Becka looked less enthused. She was not so keen, it seemed, to kill hours here instead of bodies in Bilehurst. 'Time is against us, sire, if we are to get to the village and hunt down the witches from their hiding,' she warned.

'Nah, we're fine.' Ryan peered into the box, ready to put the brakes on these bloodthirsty zealots while feigning admiration. 'I bet you have all the best kit, Your Majesty.'

Delighted, King James took the bait and took the floor: 'I have a great many artefacts – torture implements, charms, and a wide selection of body parts.' He raised a furtive eyebrow at Ryan, before making a beeline for Graham, clasping an item too big to fit in the chest, but just as treasured. 'Here, this belonged to my first Witchfinder General.'

He handed Graham a large black hat, beautifully made and oozing an austere authority. Graham took it, acting honoured, and couldn't help himself wondering how much it would fetch on *Antiques Roadshow*, while the King carried on fondly reminiscing about its previous owner.

'Scottie, who saved my life in Berwick, and later betrayed me so I had to have him shot.'

Graham's finger poked through the bullet hole. A chilling reminder of his risky new profession. Graham gulped, but James consoled him: 'I'm sure you will serve me better. You may wear the hat.'

Under pressure, Graham put it on. It was a perfect fit, and helped him play the part, blagging: 'You can trust me, sire.'

That was the wrong thing to say.

'I can trust no one! That is why I need all these,' James rasped pulling back from Graham and digging into the chest, selecting a personal favourite and turning to Ryan with a solemn smile. 'To ward off evil spirits.'

A jewelled brooch with an eye at the centre, intricate, rare, and extremely creepy. James pinned it on Ryan's coat with care, and a twinkle. 'I'll be keeping an eye on you.'

Ryan grinned as if in awe at the astonishing wit, doing whatever it took to keep the King happily distracted, and reached into the chest for a funny-looking metal tube. 'What's this?'

'Careful!' James batted him away and took the implement out, showing off his expertise, like the handler of a deadly snake. He pressed a switch on the chunky silver handle, an internal mechanism pinged, and a thick sharp needle sprang out. Thick enough to knit with, but with a far more sinister purpose. 'This is my pricker. Essential for inspections. A true witch will not bleed if her mark is pricked.' He spun around to thrust it at Becka: 'Madam, do you have one?'

For a moment, Becka was flustered, as if he meant a mark, then she realised he meant the pricker, and shook her head, wistfully prickerless. 'No, sire.'

'You may use this. It's my spare.' He handed it to her, beneficent.

Becka's fingers closed around it, grateful, and eager. 'Let us go and use it right now, sire.' Her eyes flashed with infectious fervour. James was ready to indulge her and put his toys to good use. They turned and headed for the door with the brooding Alfonso, leaving Ryan and Graham panicked, proposing an alternative plan on the hoof.

'But there's still some really, really fascinating body parts in here that you could tell us about?' Ryan struggled to keep up the front as he glimpsed what appeared to be a mummified tongue. Or possibly something grimmer.

It wasn't enough to lure James back. 'Yes, perhaps later.'

Ryan looked to Graham, desperate, as if the old guy had the handbook on waylaying monarchs from homicidal rampages.

Graham tried his best. 'Before we depart, we should make a list of all the villagers, and names of suspects, background info. It's all in the preparation.'

Ryan was impressed that Graham's mainlining of primetime crime thrillers had finally paid off, but it turned out James and Becka weren't up to speed with *CSI* whiteboards and apparently felt they had this one in the bag.

'There is no need,' Becka assured them. 'I know everything about this place, and my people.'

'And I know everything about Satan.' James stood by her; they formed a twisted double-act in the doorway, eyes ignited, unstoppable. 'Together, we will find where he is hiding, and *cut him out*. By nightfall, every last witch in this village shall be destroyed.'

9

A Golden Thread

'I've been on trial before, a couple of times,' the Doctor revealed to Yaz as they headed back through the woods to Bilehurst.

Often, Yaz thought nothing that the Doctor could say would surprise her any more, given how she'd learned to expect the unexpected, but having always cast the Doctor on the right side of justice, this one was a genuine curveball. 'You – on trial? What for?'

'Loads of stuff. The first time was for breaking a non-interference policy and I got exiled to Earth. Could've been worse.' She looked up through the tree branches, light on her face, briefly, before she darkened. 'The second time it was worse. That was for more interference, plus breaking the Laws of Time. Oh, and genocide.' She saw Yaz's surprise turn to shock and quickly added, 'I didn't do it! The evidence was faked and I was cleared of all charges, but it got pretty hairy for a while. For ages, actually. It really dragged on. And it turned out the prosecutor was kind of a future version of me, and a not very nice one, total git in fact. It's complicated.'

'Sounds like it!'

'But the point is, we can never take these things at face value. Good and evil. Innocence and guilt. There's almost always something else going on, deep down, beneath the surface.'

'Like mud tendrils? Beneath the surface … ?'

Yaz grinned, thought she might appreciate the pun, but the Doctor was in serious mode, forehead creasing in that singular way and shaking her head as she ruminated.

'That's the simplest bit. I mean motives. Why someone feels fit to pass judgment on another, to decide that God is with them and that the Devil is in the dock, when it can turn out that it's really yourself on both sides.'

Yaz grappled with the concept, struggling. 'I dunno, I've only been to court for traffic offences and urinating in a public place.' Now the Doctor was shocked so Yaz quickly added, 'To give evidence, for my job. It's all been open and shut cases so far.'

'Not any more, Yaz. Once you get past the wee cases, things get very complicated, very quickly, and justice suddenly seems less about right and wrong than rules and power. Who gets to make the laws, who gets to break them. Let's see if Willa can tell us a bit more about what's really been going down around here.'

*

The village square was deserted. Since the debacle at the ducking, the people of Bilehurst Cragg were hiding inside, for fear of witches, or Becka, or the evil in the earth. So many mysteries hung in the air, like the mist that wove out of the woods and around the silent homes.

The Doctor and Yaz tried to figure out which home might be Willa's. There was one right at the end of the village with a black cauldron outside, cold and empty, but super witchy. Wiccan charms made of sticks and feathers dangled around the door alongside bunches of drying herbs. They didn't want to pigeonhole where a suspected witch might live, but it was eerily compelling, and they were proved right as the door creaked open and Willa came out, carrying a bundle of belongings – bedding, bread, and what little money she had. Enough for somewhere to stay tonight, and after that, she was in the hands of fate. Willa didn't know fate had already found her and was hurrying over, calling.

'Willa? My name's Yaz. This is the Doctor.'

It was the witchfinders from the riverbank. The blonde one who had tried to save Granny, and the dark-haired one from the graveyard who had saved her from the beast in the dirt. They had both helped her, and yet they were witchfinders. It was confusing. This one called Yaz had a star on her clothes, like a pentacle. And the Doctor was a peculiar name for a woman, it made

59

Willa feel strange just to hear it, and the blonde woman was smiling at Willa with a warmth that somehow penetrated the bitter veil of grief that imprisoned her. Willa found herself stopping, waiting, unable to run.

'Where you going?' asked the Doctor.

'As far away from here as I can.'

'I don't blame you. But before you do, can we talk to you first? We're not witchfinders,' she said and, even though that meant she'd been lying before, it felt like she was being honest now. Like Willa might be able to trust her. 'We just want to find out exactly what's going on here and maybe we can fix things.'

Yaz nodded, encouraging. 'Will you help us, Willa? Because we wanna help you.'

Willa looked from one to the other, thinking about how her granny had helped people. Could this somehow be Granny's spirit, passed through the water, the air, into these women? How else to explain the way they made her feel – understood, ready to trust total strangers? Or was it a trick, some kind of black magic? Willa was wary, but their warmth was disarming, even as the Doctor was shivering. The cold of that river could take days to banish from your bones. Willa realised she could help the Doctor. That made her feel a little braver.

'Come inside. I've got something for you.'

While Willa lit the candles she'd just snuffed out and reheated the spiced brew on the stove until it was bubbling in the pot, the Doctor poked around, admiring the vast array of plants and herbs, dried, ground up in mortars, and then stored a mass of thick-glassed bottles. Some might call them witch's potions but the Doctor sniffed some, tasted others and understood they were medicines, nothing unnatural, created with care and a wisdom that stretched back centuries. It was less like a witch's hovel than an apothecary's shop. The scent reminded her of something that she couldn't quite place.

'Are these all yours, Willa?' The Doctor sniffed her way through the next batch.

'They were my grandmother's,' said Willa. 'She made medicines to help people. She wasn't a witch. Everyone knows that.'

Yaz sat by the stove. 'So why did Becka Savage target her?'

'Maybe she was ashamed of the woman who brought her up?' Willa divulged.

The Doctor whirled around, seizing on it: 'Wait, you and Becka are family?'

'Cousins,' Willa confided. 'We were all close till Becka married up. Left us all behind. Still, I thought we'd be safe when the witch-hunts started. Then it just got worse and worse, everyone turning on each other. Granny said it was only a matter of time before they turned on us. I didn't believe her.'

Regret balled in Willa's throat. It was hard to think back to how it all happened without cursing herself for not doing something. But what could she have done? Anything other than staying and going along with Becka's plans would have looked suspicious. Soon everything had seemed like it would look suspicious. No way could she have let on that she wept and retched before the celebration every Sunday, not when it was meant to be a joyous thing, excising the evil. Willa had felt sick for weeks now and none of the medicines helped. If she spoke up, she knew it would mean accusing someone else of causing her sickness with witchcraft. But it wasn't that. It was the witch-hunt itself, although saying such a thing could brand her a witch. No one would ever understand.

Willa forced herself to focus on the task at hand, and ladled the steaming green liquid into two earthenware mugs.

'Here – Granny's special tea. It soothes the soul.' She noted their momentary hesitation. It stung. 'Unless you think I'm a witch?'

They hastily took the mugs, took a sip. It tasted lovely, like Christmas in a cup, tingling a gingery heat from the tongue across the whole body. For the first time since the river, the Doctor could feel her fingertips and toes again. However it struck her that, out of the three of them, Willa looked like she needed her soul soothing most of all.

'Are you not having any?'

'I feel too sick.'

That reminded the Doctor. 'Do you mind if I check you over? Don't worry, I am a doctor.' She pulled out her sonic.

Willa pulled back, on edge as the sonic lit up and whirred. 'What's that?'

'Specialist equipment,' the Doctor didn't really explain, sensing any explanation would only lead to more questions and they were on the clock to get to the tendril. She trusted that her authoritative tone would sell it and started to scan Willa, who let her, but found the sickness in her stomach churning again with the latest worries.

'That movement in the mud, that was Satan, wasn't it?

'Doubt it.' The Doctor checked the sonic – nothing special coming up – and tried again. 'Not a big believer in Satan.' Again, she could have elaborated, about the time she spent wrestling with a certain Beast in a certain pit, but again, it wouldn't help matters. That Beast had no business with the mud in Bilehurst, and Willa needed reassurance.

It worked. Willa nodded, fondly remembering: 'My granny used to say there were enough wonders in nature without making things up.'

'I like your granny,' the Doctor smiled as she double-checked. Still nothing. 'Completely normal. No magic – not that I believe in that either, it's just a catch-all for weird stuff – and no signs of any sickness.'

Willa clutched her stomach 'You're wrong.'

'I think I know what it is that's making you sick.' Yaz diagnosed her, not as a doctor or a detective, but as someone who might just have been in a similar boat. Yaz had been watching Willa and seen enough to recognise the signs. She'd lived with them herself for long enough, long ago. No one else had ever known about it, until now. 'I had it, at my school where I'm from, when Izzy Flint turned the whole class against me. Every day I'd wake up feeling this dread, fear.'

Yaz flashed back to those school days, aching to stay at home, but unable to hurt her family by revealing the truth, and knowing any absence would only make things worse when she returned. Because Izzy would seek her out and make her pay twice as much, or more. Sometimes it was physical, a punch or a kick or a fistful of Yaz's hair pulled out, which was painful, but much easier to deal with than the looks, the words, the public humiliation.

The worst was in the changing rooms for PE, when Yaz's kit had vanished from her bag and she was forced to wear the spares from lost property. No one would come near her at Izzy's behest, all laughing that Yaz couldn't afford the kit, that she stank, that she didn't belong there and should go back where she came from. None of it was true and everyone knew it, but no one dared stand up to Izzy in case she turned her spotlight on them. So they ganged up on Yaz, leaving her to get picked last for teams, never throwing her the ball and flinching away when she came close. It would build up through the lesson so by the time they went back to the changing room, the games were just beginning. They stole her uniform and threw it between them like a vicious spin on netball with Yaz trying to grab it back and the girls blocking her, tossing her clothes around until they were torn and filthy, and she couldn't hold the tears back any longer. Maybe Izzy was right in a way – Yaz definitely didn't belong there, in this vortex of pain and rage and hate, but there was no escape.

This flash took a nanosecond but it stabbed deep into Yaz's guts, conjuring the phantom of that sickness again. Willa felt it, recognised it instantly, riveted, hoping for answers. 'How did you get rid of it?'

'I didn't.' Not the answer that Willa was hoping for, but Yaz stood up, held her glance, empathic with this Northern girl going through tough times, feeling alone. 'I just took it, had the year from hell. When I say hell, I don't literally mean hell – I mean it was really awful. It stuck with me for a long time after, really got me down, which made me even more of a target. One day, I ran away. Scares me to think how I might've ended up. But someone good stopped me, made me see there was another way. And I told myself, some day I'd stand up to the Izzy Flints of this world.'

There was the hope. A golden thread spun by Yaz, stretching out to Willa if she was willing to take hold of it, keep weaving. Willa wanted to, but the fear gripped too hard. Painful, paralysing, warping the world so she distrusted all her instincts.

'I can't stand up to Becka. She'll have me tried for a witch.' Willa's eyes filled at the futility of it all. 'What am I meant to do?'

The Doctor laid it out. 'Seems to me like you have two choices. Run, as far away from here as possible. Or stick with us. We'll stand up to Becka Savage, and we'll make this place safe again.

'How will we do that?'

The Doctor beamed: 'Ah! We. That's good, Willa. See? It feels better already.'

Willa was about to protest, explain that was not what she'd meant. What she'd meant was to dismiss the idea that they could do anything to defeat Becka and make this place safe. The whole notion was unthinkable. But suddenly she realised – the sickness had eased. When she thought about 'we' and 'us' instead of 'I' and 'me', the dread seemed to shrink. How did the Doctor do that? With the specialist equipment? Was it some kind of magic? Was Yaz's story a kind of spell? If this was witchcraft, surely it had to be good.

The Doctor was already moving on, pacing around the room and talking fast, no time to waste. 'Now, first things first, I need to get a sample of that mud. Can I use this?' She grabbed an empty bottle.

Willa nodded. The Doctor liked her more and more. 'Wanna come with us?'

Willa looked at her bundle, considered still running away. The 'we' and 'us' were good, but what use were they against the power of Becka? Let alone against that devil in the dirt. Willa answered honestly.

'Not really.'

But she knew she that would. That she'd follow these two women wherever fate led them, connected not by fear now, but by that fine and fragile golden thread of hope.

10

Digging in the Dirt

Ryan and Graham followed the royal party, hotfooting it through the wintry woods, trying desperately to slow their progress. Ryan jogged up ahead to seduce James into slowing down while Graham went to tackle Becka.

'Oy oy, hold up, what's the rush?' He trotted alongside Becka, who had left home so fast she'd forgotten to wear her cape. Her skin goose-bumped and her breath fogged in the icy air.

'I want this over. So that we can return to the way things were before Satan infested this land.'

Graham took her arm, gently but firmly made her stop, hoping the hat and some attitude would help him get to the bottom of this.

'Excuse me, but when you say Satan, what exactly do you mean?'

'Satan is all around us. All of the time. We must be strong or else he will take us. Of that I have no doubt.' There was true fear in her eyes. She believed every word. But Graham couldn't quite believe Becka.

'Really? No doubt? But what if you're wrong? Cos you're killing all these people – friends, neighbours.'

'If people are good, they have nothing to fear.'

Such vague statements didn't wash with this Witchfinder General. Graham locked eyes with her, made it personal. 'Are you a good person, Mistress Savage?'

She held his look, no flicker of doubt. 'My conscience is clean.' She pulled her arm back and marched on. Graham was frustrated, hoped that Ryan was having more luck.

Alfonso strode up ahead, out to prove his prowess over the new pretender. Ryan hung back, trying to settle the King into more of a stroll and draw out some of his longer anecdotes. He had already endured James's musings on *Macbeth*, apparently based on a true story tinkered with by Shakespeare to flatter the King. Banquo was inspired by one of James's ancestors and was therefore the only wise and good man in the play, able to see the truth where others were blinded by ambition and other mortal weaknesses. The three witches' prophecy that that the heirs of Banquo would gain the throne of Scotland helped to bolster James's claim and his confidence that no usurper could take his power. But it was a strange confidence, this utter certainty in his divine right, coupled with a raging insecurity that it could all fall away at any moment. Ryan also found it odd that James set so much store by the witches' prophecy, given his patent dislike of witches. When he'd pointed that out, there was an awkward silence and James sped up, leaving Ryan floundering, forced to big up Alfonso in a bid to get the King talking again.

'Alfonso seems like a good guy to have around, sire. Very handy with that sword, I bet?'

'With his pistol too, not to mention his fists.' James took the cue, witch hypocrisy swiftly erased by Alfonso appreciation. 'Look at him. Alfonso's loyalty is rare and pure, but it's only a matter of time before I inevitably get let down.'

His insecurity erased even the fondness for Alfonso. Ryan didn't get it, why the most powerful guy in the land was so insecure. He knew it was the same back in the present day, with rulers from the president down to his sadistic shift manager at the warehouse, but he didn't get why and he wanted to know.

'Why do you find it so hard to trust people?'

'It's a long sad story. A tragedy.' James chuckled, but a genuine sadness undercut it.

'I've got time. Tell me?'

Ryan stopped to listen and to his relief the King stopped too, all the better to hold his young audience, rapt. But this was not just another anecdote, it was a painful truth, rarely voiced. James took a moment to find the right way in.

'My father died when I was a baby.'

'I feel you,' Ryan nodded, heartfelt. 'I lost my mum, and my nan.'

'My father was murdered by my mother, who was then imprisoned and beheaded.'

'OK, that's worse.' What else could Ryan say? This was a whole other league, although on reflection he figured it might have the same dumbfounding effect on James if Ryan said his nan had died falling off a crane after being electrocuted while battling an alien gathering coil. Perhaps best not to get into that. Just keep listening, empathising.

'I was raised by regents. One was assassinated. One died in battle. And another died in suspicious circumstances. There have been numerous attempts to kidnap me, kill me, or blow me up. It's a miracle I'm still alive.'

'You're not kidding!' Ryan exclaimed. Not the most empathetic response, but he was seriously out of his depth here.

'No, I'm not. It is a miracle that I have prevailed, whilst all around me others fall.'

A miracle. So that's what James had placed his faith in. That his life would be under constant threat and each attempt needed a last-minute miracle to save him. Alfonso was just window-dressing. Nothing could really make James feel safe and secure. But maybe Ryan could play on that insecurity, find a way to parlay it into a swift exit for the King.

'You should definitely get yourself back to London, sire. Keep yourself safe.'

After all, he looked around at the eerie woods, this was not the place for miracles. But James's face took on a beatific light as he declared: 'God will keep me safe, as long as I do his work.' He cast a glance to the heavens, as if to reconfirm the deal, and then exhaled. 'Ooh, that felt good! Thank you,' he chuckled. 'And now we can have some fun, aye, Ryan?'

With a flick of his wrist, James pinged his pricker and strode off to hunt with a fresh vigour, re-energised thanks to Ryan reminding him of his mission. Ryan kicked himself. He and Graham had clawed back a few minutes, but the murderers were more determined than ever. He really hoped the Doctor and Yaz were having more luck.

The earth from Mother Twiston's grave still lay heaped in a pile, just as Willa had left it when the tendril attacked. The Doctor scanned every inch, searching for any trace of alien matter, but it eluded her.

'It's just mud. No sign of any tendency to tendril. I shouldn't be disappointed but I am a bit.' She kept searching, refining the settings to go deeper, just in case the blighter was hiding in the foggy sub-molecular level. The problem with mud tendrils was that they could be anything from the tendrils of a vast squid-like mud beast to no beast at all, just a force manipulating the mud in this instance. If the former, that could be a nice straightforward barney, but the latter could have moved on to manipulating sticks, rocks or badgers by now. Which was its own kind of fun, but much harder to isolate.

Yaz picked up the dropped spade and kept hold of it, just in case the tendril came back. She had her own line of investigation to pursue with Willa, getting her to open up. 'What was that ritual you were doing before the tendril arrived?'

'A prayer. To help my granny rest in peace. I brought her body here, I dug that grave, and placed her in it. But I didn't get to finish the prayer.' That lump in her throat again, the grief still raw despite the distractions of the mud beast hunt. Yaz understood.

'We can finish it now, if you like?'

Willa nodded, grateful, and turned to look for the holly wreath.

'Right, little sample, what aren't you telling me?' Getting no love from scanning the mud en masse, the Doctor had put a small lump it into the glass bottle. Her intention was to take it back to the TARDIS and subject it to some hardcore assessments, but that plan went out of the window as, the moment she corked the bottle, the mud suddenly twitched, smoothed itself into a ball and started racing around the bottle, tinging into the sides of the glass like an angry wasp. The Doctor's face lit up like a lottery winner.

'Whoa! I am no longer disappointed.'

Yaz beamed, vindicated. 'See? The mud is alive.'

'Well, now I'm not sure it's mud at all.' The Doctor monitored its movements, fascinated. This was definitely down the manipulative force end of the spectrum, but what sort of force and what was it doing in a witches' graveyard in Pendle in 1612?

'It looks pretty angry in there,' Yaz ventured.

'Yaz?' A tremble in Willa's voice drew Yaz's attention back from the bottle. She turned to see what the matter was.

'It doesn't like being trapped, do you?' Ever optimistic, the Doctor liked to give new acquaintances a chance to communicate civilly before resorting to the sonic. It might be angry, but who wouldn't be, being imprisoned in a bottle out of the blue? 'What are you? Give us a clue.'

'What's happening?' Willa asked Yaz, the tremble in her voice clearly terror now, but Yaz just stared stunned, and the Doctor thought everyone was still as fixated with the little mud guy as she was.

'I think this is some kind of alien matter, but I'm not sure if it's sentient.'

'Doctor, park that please?' Yaz tried to keep it together so Willa wouldn't freak.

'Why?' The Doctor turned and saw what they were staring at, realised why her mud guy had been eclipsed in the billing.

Mother Twiston had risen from the grave.

11

Witchcraft!

Mother Twiston stood by her open grave, undead. Her shroud had been clawed off, leaving her standing in a filthy smock, wet from the river and coated in clumps of mud. Dirt streaked her hair, caked on her face, stained her skin, and it was even in her eyes, the whites swimming with dark gritty liquid. She was a terrifying sight, all the more so because her face was no otherworld monster but a kindly old woman who Willa loved more than anything on Earth. She had the red berries from the wreath scattered in her hair, clinging to her grubby clothes. Willa's prayer had been answered – Mother Twiston was still with her, but no thanks to air or fire or any natural force in this world.

'Granny?' Willa cried out.

'That is not your granny, Willa.' The Doctor got between them, in case Willa got any ill-advised urges to go and check for herself. Emotions and beliefs easily clouded the stark evidence of this creature's oozing inhumanity.

'Yes it is,' Willa insisted, tormented by the vision and her conflicting impulses – to run and hug her granny or to run away screaming.

'No, that's the – not-mud – some sort of alien matter filling her body and reanimating it. So it is pretty sentient. I'm so sorry for this, Willa,' said the Doctor.

Mother Twiston was moving around the grave towards them, slowly, a jerking motion, as if the not-mud was learning to use this new body it inhabited. It was a fast learner, staggering to face the Doctor, who stayed put, up for a confrontation to find out more, hopefully without too much antagonism.

'Hi, Not-Willa's-Granny. I presume you're just using the body to give whatever you are form? Better than tendrils, right? But really not right. Not cool.'

Mother Twiston looked her up and down with undead earth eyes. Not cool at all.

'Is that why it went after Willa?' Yaz asked, trying to get her head around this.

'Of course! Not to kill her, but to fill her. Oh – check out my rhymes, poetry under pressure.' The Doctor took time out from the terror, trying to lighten the mood. Futile.

There was a low gurgle from inside Mother Twiston, like mud in her guts, in her throat. She looked like she was trying to speak, or perhaps projectile-vomit black mud all over them.

The Doctor backed off, wary, while continuing the inquisition. 'What're you doing?' The old woman's mud-crusted hands reached out, nails dripping with dirt, grasping towards … the bottle? That could make a certain sense.

'You want this? One of you, is it? Or part of you?'

As the Doctor held the bottle up to ascertain if she was right, Mother Twiston made a grab for it. Theory confirmed, the Doctor yanked it away, out of reach.

'Oh no you don't, not until you tell me what's going on here,' she laid down the law. If the mud could learn to walk and manifest its desires, it could learn to explain itself too. In the meantime, she got a closer look at the hands, mud spewing out through the pores in their palms. It had infiltrated every part of Mother Twiston and still wanted more.

'I don't like the look of this. It's all bubbling away inside you.'

Mother Twiston made another grab for the bottle. Could that mud fill her and Yaz and Willa too? Just from a few drops, no tendril required? The Doctor wasn't going to take that risk.

'Oh no, you're not filling me like a mud bath. If you're that desperate for it – here!'

She tossed the bottle to Mother Twiston, who snatched it out of the air and crushed it in her muddy palm, oblivious to the shards of glass in her flesh, focused on the mud ball. She gobbled it up, smacking her lips. So she felt no pain and was strong and hungry. The Doctor assessed her, both repulsed and fascinated by the biology. 'Delightful. Down the hatch!'

Mother Twiston licked her filthy fingers, like that was just for starters. Fascination still had the edge on repulsion, so the Doctor stuck with it, sure that the creature would find its tongue sooner or later.

'I have got so many questions right now, like, did you drink that? Or absorb it? Are you all one big muddy mass or separate entities, only taking the one body?'

'Doctor?'

There was no mistaking the terror in Yaz's voice this time. And rightly so, because this time when the Doctor turned to look, she saw the reanimated bodies of four more undead mud-witches risen from the freshest graves.

'Always good to get fast answers,' the Doctor said, endeavouring to keep things light. What else was there to do in the face of encroaching hell?

Willa had a much more normal response. She screamed.

The scream echoed through the woods. Graham and Ryan swapped worried looks.

'What was that?' James gasped with excitement, witchfinder instincts jangling.

Becka sounded more scared than excited. 'I cannot imagine.'

'Erm, best let us deal with this, sire,' said Graham, trying to take the lead and keep their charges away from any action.

Ryan joined him, insisting: 'You should stay here where it's safe, sire.'

But James was having none of it. 'Nowhere is safe, until Satan has been vanquished!' Before they could stop him, the King charged off in the direction of the scream, a glint in his eye and his pricker held aloft, ready for action.

'Er, did it come from that way, sire? I thought it came from the other way.' A valiant effort from Graham, but James wasn't listening to anyone – except the higher calling that urged him on. Alfonso scampered after him, followed by Becka and her guards. Graham and Ryan looked at each other, dreading to think what carnage was about to unfold, but running towards it anyway.

The Doctor, Yaz and Willa looked like three witches, huddled amongst the graves with a brood of rotting muddy corpses, lurching towards them. The Doctor held them at bay with the sonic, but it wouldn't take them long to figure out she couldn't harm them with it. Despite the black clouds in their eyes, there was an intelligence at work in there, and the Doctor wasn't sure how long she could bamboozle it with lights and sounds.

'Stay back, please!'

She got the wooden cart between herself, Yaz and Willa and the five mud-witches. Apart from Mother Twiston, the other four were young women. Even now, despite the death and the dirt, there was an eerie beauty to them, a sadness from their wasted lives, cut short by Becka's purge. None of them had been witches in life, but they were bewitching now, reaching out to their living sisters. Mud drooled from their lips, dripping from their rancid hands, and leaking like black tears from their matted lashes.

The Doctor ramped up the volume on the sonic, but still the mud-witches kept closing in.

Willa was clearly fighting to keep hold of her fear. Yaz clutched hold of her arm. 'Remember, it's not your granny. It's not the people you used to know. That mud is using their bodies …'

The Doctor glowered at the creatures. 'I've given you the blob, what more do you need?' More bodies, if she had to guess, but it bugged her having to guess when they could just fess up. 'So annoying when they're silent.'

'Witchcraft!'

As if she didn't have enough to deal with, the Doctor saw James dashing in, cape flying, pricker primed. Alfonso was at his side, sword drawn, and the rest of the crew soon came running up behind, including Graham and Ryan signalling their slightly sheepish apologies.

'So much for keeping that lot at the house,' the Doctor muttered, put out.

'Stay where you are!' King James commanded, under the illusion that he was still in charge here.

The Doctor waved at him, from the far side of the mud-witch contingent that stood between them. 'Hi, sire, I know it looks bad, but don't worry, I'm all over it.' She sonicked some more, disco-settings, last chance to keep them distracted.

Becka was pale, pointing her finger, convinced: 'Willa Twiston was the witch all along, I knew it.'

'I'm not!' Willa shouted. 'This isn't me, Becka, I swear.'

'She's right,' the Doctor snapped. 'It's not her and it's not witchcraft. I'm working it out.'

'This is beyond you, woman,' James dismissed her. 'Alfonso, shoot them!'

'Of course, Your Majesty.' Alfonso tossed sword aside and pulled out his pistol.

The Doctor's hearts plummeted as she saw Mother Twiston turn. A gun was never good, but in this case the Doctor had a particularly bad feeling about it. 'No, Alfonso, don't!'

A voice from inside Mother Twiston, rasping and claggy, rigor-mortised vocal cords lubricated by gushing alien mud, raising the spectre of the dead woman's final words: 'In the air and in the earth!'

Any satisfaction from the pay-off that the creatures were capable of speech was dwarfed by the Doctor's horror as the five witches raised their hands as one, reaching towards the young man with the pistol and releasing a blastwave that smashed into his body with the force of several trucks. Alfonso hurtled backwards, dead before he hit the ground. The pistol fell in the dirt beside him.

'Alfonso!' James cried out, reeling.

The Doctor was fuming. All five mud-witches were moving as a unit now, towards them, with nefarious intent. She knew there would be no negotiating. 'Now you've made them angry. They're getting stronger. Get away from here now!'

The witches raised their hands to strike again. The Doctor grabbed Yaz and Willa, and ran, herding everyone else ahead of them as fast as she could, into the woods.

12

Guilt

'This way, through here.' The Doctor led the way, racing through the trees, into a clearing. A chance to catch their breath and check how close the mud-witches were behind them. The mist wasn't so thick that she couldn't see a good distance, but she couldn't see anything moving. Apart from their panting little band – the Doctor, Yaz, Ryan, Graham, Willa, Becka, James and the two guards – the woods seemed deserted.

'I don't think they're following us,' Yaz confirmed, frowning.

'If they're not following us, what are they doing?' the Doctor wondered to herself, unnerved.

'Want us to go and look?' Ryan gamely volunteered.

James sputtered, incredulous: 'We escape from Satan and you wish to go directly back into battle?'

'We need to know what they're up to.' Ryan was already setting off, energised. 'Make sure no one else is in danger.'

Graham stepped up: 'I'll go too. Keep an eye on my underlings.'

Yaz and Ryan shot Graham a look as they headed off on their mud-witch-finding mission. He was enjoying that hat a bit too much now.

'I'll stay with Willa. Be careful!' the Doctor called after them. She needed to know what those mud-witches were up to, but James and Becka were equally deadly and she wasn't leaving Willa to fend for herself. Besides, where Ryan and Graham had failed to subdue the maniacal pair, she was sure she could make more inroads. After the encounter in the graveyard, they'd have to see that killing more innocent women wasn't the way forward. Could that cruelty even be the very thing that was somehow causing this mud alien phenomenon? The Doctor's mind wanted to race on through all the possibilities, but was dragged back to basics by the King, who was over the initial hit of adrenalin and terror, and now sank down onto a tree stump, bereft, trying to make sense of it all.

'What were those aberrations?'

'It was the work of Satan,' Becka assured him.

The Doctor assured him otherwise. 'It wasn't Satan, or witches, or Willa's granny. Those creatures were being controlled by something in the mud, something not of this Earth, something beyond your understanding.'

'Something from hell?' James at least seemed willing to listen and learn, albeit within a frustratingly narrow frame of reference. She wondered if he could help her figure it out, if she could talk in his terms?

'More like from the heavens. They chose to kill Alfonso when he was a threat, but in other circumstances it fills the bodies and uses them as vessels. I don't know why. Maybe only when they're dead?'

'No, it attacked me too,' Willa reminded her.

Becka looked between them, pale and mute, sticking by her satanic analysis with the total absence of doubt that had frustrated Graham and frankly bamboozled the Doctor. Never in all her incarnations could the Doctor ever recall experiencing such an absolute certainty, unhindered by lack of evidence or rigorous questioning. Even the Doctor's belief in love and hope and all that good stuff was inherently riven with doubt. That was why it required faith. But not Becka's kind of blind faith. The day the Doctor stopped asking questions would likely be the day she ceased to regenerate. As for now, the questions flowed thick and fast as she paced around the clearing, trying to clarify.

'Why today? Because this is my problem – I can buy that this is the biggest ever witch-hunt in England. Or I can buy it's an alien mud invasion. But both on the same day? I can't buy that. Oh wait – unless they're connected. Your witch-hunt's been going on a while now, so there's no way that mud has just rocked up today. What do you know, Becka? What's going on here in Bilehurst Cragg?'

All eyes were on Becka, James's thinning with suspicion. Becka was still mute, panicked by the accusation she perceived, because she assumed the Doctor was like her, pointing the finger, not simply trying to figure this out. She stepped back as the Doctor advanced, firing a more threatening question.

'A woman who keeps an axe under her bed – what have you seen?'

Finally Becka spoke, with utter self-possession: 'I have seen you, with your wand, raising your kin from the dead.'

Now the Doctor was dumbstruck. And James's suspicions swung around, throwing the spotlight on the Doctor as she floundered.

'What? No! Hold on a sec …'

James rose from his tree-stump, reinvigorated by Becka's breakthrough: 'You are no witchfinder's assistant. You are Satan's acolyte.'

'I am not!'

All that time Becka was silent, it seemed she had been preparing her case. Statements, not questions, skilfully constructed to convince King James of her vision. Now she pointed her finger: 'That is why it's happening today. Because you are here. As you say – to take over this village!'

'You know that's not what I meant. We do not have time for this,' the Doctor argued.

The pricker pinged once more as the King moved towards the Doctor, the lethal point gleaming: 'Mistress Savage is correct. It is your fault that Alfonso is dead.'

The Doctor understood his grief, the need to blame someone for Alfonso's death, someone other than the King himself, seeing as he was the one responsible. She was too tactful to say that, but she had to point out: 'I tried to save him.'

'You saved *them*, from being shot!' James stuck with his own logic, racking up the evidence. 'You said this evil fell from the heavens. Oh yes it fell, like your lord – Lucifer!'

The Doctor rolled her eyes at the heavens, more exasperated than scared by their idiotic accusations: 'Honestly, if I was still a bloke, I could get on with the job and not have to waste time defending myself!'

'Oh you bewitch us with your alluring form and incessant jabber, but I knew you were unnatural from the very start, and now I see you for what you really are. *A witch.*'

It wasn't until then that the Doctor grasped the gravity of what was happening here. In a few words, she'd gone from being cheesed off at the stupidity of seventeenth-century sexism to truly understanding the risks of this new body she inhabited. That it didn't just bring new obstacles. It could very easily get her killed if she wasn't careful. The exasperation took a backseat to fear. The kind of fear she'd sworn wouldn't be an issue for her, because she was a kick-ass Gallifreyan travelling the galaxies, not a chick getting chatted up at a bar or walking home down a dark alley. But it turned out time had played its tricks with her and it only took a moment for all her powers to vanish, so that suddenly she was seen as 'just a woman' in the presence of powerful forces with evil intent.

Willa felt it too, and had to force herself to speak up. An hour ago she was too scared to stand up to Becka and now here she was arguing the toss with the King. She knew it was a risk, but Yaz's story emboldened her. 'She was trying to save us, sire.'

'Thank you, Willa!' The girl's bravery, in turn, emboldened the Doctor. That was how this worked. Women bigged each other up and the patriarchy came crumbling down. That was how it was meant to work anyway.

Becka apparently hadn't got that memo. She stepped in between them, cutting the connection and appealing to Willa. 'Are you sure you're not mistaken, Willa? Or are you in league with the witches as I first suspected?'

There it was, the threat of accusation, no mistaking. Willa felt it, knew she was next if she didn't choose the right side. But it wasn't so clear to her which side that was.

'She said she wanted to help me.'

'Who do you trust to save you? Your King, your family?' Becka amped up the pressure, pivoting from cruel accuser to caring cousin – and magnanimous landowner. 'Whatever I have done, I did to save all of our souls.'

The Doctor stared at Becka, half in awe of this woman's sheer bravura in twisting the truth, and half besieged by more questions, because this wasn't pure ignorance she was detecting in Becka. There was fleet-footed intelligence to it, suggesting a deeper motive. That dark alley of investigation was so compelling, the Doctor almost forgot to keep being scared as she ventured another question. The only question.

'What's really going on, Becka?'

'Hold your tongue or I will cut it out,' James snapped, and it had the desired effect, silencing the Doctor with fear once again. She had no doubt that he would action it right there and then, rip through it with his pricker in the name of goodness and truth, taking away her greatest weapon, her words. James only wanted answers to his own questions. He turned to Willa, severe enough to ward her off standing up to him again.

'Well? Tell the truth, lassie!'

He waited, impatient. Becka's eyes bored into Willa, warning her that there was only one acceptable truth to tell. Willa looked at the Doctor, despairing. Willa had known her less than a day, while Becka had been there since Willa was born, and the King was everywhere – on coins and in paintings and pamphlets and books. He made the Bible! How could she trust this strange new woman over that, no matter what her heart was telling her? No matter that the dread pain was already surging back into her belly at the thought of letting the Doctor down. Willa's eyes filled. This was impossible.

James was sick of waiting. He nodded, urging Willa to confess and save her eternal soul. Speak now or burn in hell forever.

Willa found some words which weren't a lie, so she could tell the truth without too much regret. 'I did think it was strange, when they said her name was the Doctor.'

It was a small thing. Willa hoped it would be enough to make them stop grilling her, but not enough to incriminate the Doctor. She was half-right.

'Like Doctor Dee – a necromancer!' James gasped. 'That seals it. Arrest the witch!'

Before Willa dared to protest, the guards grabbed the Doctor and dragged her away. The Doctor kicked and tried to fight them off, but they could snap her bones in an instant and would be happy to do so, so she had to submit and settle for yelling in vague hopes her friends would hear, but mostly from pure rage at the universe for making her suffer this way at this point in time 'I'm not a witch!'

No one listened except Willa, who felt the truth of those words like a knife in the belly, adding a potent new ingredient to the toxic mix of grief and fear swilling inside. Guilt.

13

Failure

Time is running out. The sun is rising. The guards will be coming for me soon. Doctor, can you not hear me?

Or have you not forgiven me for betraying you to Becka and King James? Do you want me to know how it feels? To be wrongly accused, denied, dragged off, imprisoned?

I don't blame you if that is the case. The look on your face as I gave the damning evidence against you – the disappointment, that cut deep. But you don't want me to die for it, do you? I deserve to suffer for it, but think what I'd been through that day, how scared I was. You were incredible, but this was the King, and my cousin, the only family I had left. And if I hadn't said what they wanted, they'd have killed me too. Is that why I deserve to die now? Because if I had done the right thing, I would be dead already? Perhaps there is some justice in that. But it doesn't feel like the Doctor's justice. Perhaps you are just leaving it until the last moment, to make your dashing entrance, to rescue me.

You had better hurry. I can hear the guards' footsteps. I have to stop writing, and hide this in the wall, behind the brick I loosened, only to find many more bricks behind. Perhaps one day you'll find this and read it and at least bring my memory to life, so someone will know the end of my story. Or perhaps no one will read it and no one will care. The witch is dead.

14

Discoveries of Witches

Graham and his underlings didn't hear the Doctor's cry of rage. They were too far away, combing the woods for any trace of the mud-witches, but apart from the flutter and caw of a lonely raven, the place seemed deserted. Had the dead women gone back to earth?

'Have a look over here.' Graham spotted something, crouched down to peer in the dirt.

Ryan and Yaz came to see, tentative in case of tendrils, but these were smaller, brighter.

'Holly berries,' Graham said with a gravitas befitting his hat. Ryan didn't see the significance until Graham added, 'But there's no holly trees here.'

They looked around, not knowing the names of the bare hawthorns, rowans and sycamores that surrounded them, but seeing none of them had prickly green leaves. Hence these little giveaways must have fallen from the witches' hair and clothes as they walked this way. Yaz grinned, excited, and spotted more scattered in the leaf mulch.

'They can't be far. Come on.'

They followed the trail of blood-red drips through the forest, like Hansel and Gretel and an old witchfinder they'd brought along to help them track down the gingerbread house. There was nothing so sweet and cosy in these woods, but before long, Graham spotted movement in the mist. He pulled Yaz and Graham behind a dried-up tangle of briers to hide and watch, breaths held, as the mud-witches emerged out of the murk.

Mother Twiston led the way, flanked by the younger four in a V-formation like migrating mud-slicked birds, seeming to instinctively know the route. There was clear intent as they picked up the pace, and their leaking black eyes glinted with purpose. Behind them, their hands stretched and twitched, fingers flexing, claw-like, as if the mud was flooding the tips and needed somewhere else to go, someone else to flow into.

Yaz shuddered as she watched them, reminding herself that until recently most had been girls like her, subjected to a hideous death and now dragged into something worse. Despite her fears, it fired her up to find out more and find a way to bring them peace. She nodded to Graham and whispered, impressed.

'You should take up witchfinding for a living.'

'Yeah, shame I missed the training sesh on what to do when you've found them,' Graham sighed.

'I guess we have to follow them,' Ryan bit the bullet. 'Very quietly.'

They waited until the witches were at a safe distance – although who really knew what the radius of the witches' senses was, or how fast they could move, or even if they could animate the mud underfoot? Yaz took a deep breath and hoped for the best as she crept out from behind the briar and followed Ryan's advice, followed him and Graham, following the mud-witches, very quietly, into the gloom.

The sun was sinking fast, casting eerie shadows across the village square, where the party atmosphere was a distant memory. The only show in town was the Doctor, tied up to a sturdy post by her wrists, like a criminal in the stocks ready to be pilloried and pelted. People were welcome to have a go, but no one dared. This Doctor was clearly different to the common witches from the village. She was dangerous, and only the armed guards and a few chilled-out geese dared go anywhere near. The Doctor felt she'd have more luck winning over the geese than the guards and that was saying something, because the geese were supremely disinterested in her plight, but finally King James approached and the Doctor summoned up some hope. James might be responsible for her current predicament, but he was a mercurial man and if she could just find the right way to enlighten him, his allegiance would give her the freedom to take on that alien muck and make this place safe again before daylight failed. She had a very bad feeling about being stuck here at night with James, Becka and a bunch of deadly undead mud-witches.

'Comfortable, witch? I do hope not.'

'Come for a visit?' She was aiming for cheerful, but couldn't quite get there, riled by the way he strolled in like he owned the joint. OK, so he did technically own it at this point in history, but being across many other points made his posturing seem even more silly and irrelevant and wasting her time. She tried to bite all that back and hear him out.

'I will take my chance to converse with an agent of Satan,' James said grandly, circling her.

'If I was Satan's agent, do you seriously think a bit of rope would stop me? I say a bit, there's quite a lot. Tightly bound. It's pretty painful. They know how to tie a knot in this part of the world!'

Too cheery. She would have to split the difference. Find some common ground between republicanism, land rights and Northern nodeology. Luckily he dismissed the knot talk and leaned in, eyes glittering as he surveyed his prize prisoner.

'I am an expert on witchcraft, Doctor. But I wish to learn more. Before you die, I want answers.'

OK, this she could work with. The Doctor was a big fan of the Socratic method for any subject, even Satanism. She remembered now that James's *Dæmonologie* was itself in the form of a dialogue debating the dos and don'ts of all things demonic. To be fair, neither of those characters was playing the Devil's advocate so James hadn't quite got the hang of maximising Q&As, but it was a promising start. It meant he was still open to absorbing new information, new realities beyond the beliefs that blinkered him.

Before she could get stuck in and set the agenda, he whipped the sonic out from under his cape and thrust it at her, challenging. 'Your wand, how does it work?'

She toyed with offering to show him, but he wasn't that dim. She had to hope he was smart, treat him that way and let him rise to the challenge. Plus her method always worked better when she asked instead of answered. 'Why do you want to know?'

'I wish to know all the secrets of existence.'

'Don't we all? But true knowledge has to be earned.' She saw he didn't like that, clocked his knuckles whitening around the wand. She wanted her sonic back so badly she took a chance. 'Tell you what, I'll trade you my wand for answers to as many questions as you want to ask.'

Nope, bad idea. Definitely the kind of line an imp of Satan would come out with. James stashed the sonic away and puffed out his chest. 'I'm not a fool, Doctor. I am King James, Satan's greatest foe—'

'Yeah, yeah, I know. It must be comforting playing that role. Hiding behind a title.'

'Just as you hide behind "Doctor", perhaps?'

Now they were talking. Now she could ask. 'Who are you, really? Behind the mask, the drama. What does it say on your garter?'

She looked down, to a blue velvet band around his leg, delicately embroidered in gold with the motto of the Chivalric Order of the Garter.

'*Honi soit qui mal y pense,*' James answered in a perfect French accent with a flourish of pride, as if it had been a purely factual question. It was just the start.

'Evil be to him that evil thinks,' she translated. James nodded, like, *duh!* The Doctor shook her head and let him have it. 'You wear it like a hero, even though you're killing and scapegoating and stirring up hate. And you wonder why the darkness comes back at you?'

James recoiled, affronted: 'There is no darkness in me. I quest for goodness and knowledge, beauty and art, all of God's virtues.'

'Your own mother was scapegoated,' she shot back. 'How do you square that with your witch-hunts?'

His face changed, the mask falling. His voice filled with barely suppressed emotion: 'What do you know of my mother?'

The Doctor knew a lot, as much as anyone, from the facts side of things at least, but which should she use to peel more layers away from James, to get him to understand? She thought of his mother's letters to him, when she was under house arrest. Here he was, fraternising with an evil witch prisoner who he barely knew, but he only ever wrote to his mother, never got anywhere near this close. So what really scared James? And would he ever admit it?

'You could have seen her before she died, but you didn't want to. Why?'

Pain flashed across his face, another layer seared off. 'She left me, when I was not even one year old. What kind of mother does that? Why would I wish to see her?'

The Doctor softened, but kept pushing, gentle yet firm: 'Nobody will ever know why she left you, James. But you can't go hurting people just because you're scared to face up to the darkness inside you. You have to be better than that.'

It was working. She was getting to him. He sat down on a log, no longer posturing, more like the lost little boy he'd once been, trembling as he looked up at her. 'Who are you? How do you know these things?'

'I know because we're all the same. We want certainty, security, to believe that people are evil or heroic, but that's not how people are. You want to know the secrets of existence? Start with the mysteries of the heart,' she implored him, reaching out even while her hands were tied, with her words, her trust. 'I could show you everything, if you stop being afraid of what you don't understand. If you trust me.' The biggest ask, she knew, but she could feel him longing, wavering, so she

103

laid it out. 'I am not a witch. But if you want to defeat evil, you have to let me go now. Please, sire?'

They locked eyes. He looked like he would, like he understood, like he might just trust himself and reach out to meet her, release her. But then – she could see the fear flit across his face, a protective layer shuttering up as the thought struck him – he felt like she was good, but that could itself be evidence of her trickery. How could anyone of this Earth make him feel like this? Argue him around to the opposite position, as if he had been wrong all along? That couldn't be right. And even if it was, he couldn't just trust to feelings or even logic. Socrates had his limits. James needed a more scientific method. Just to be sure.

'I do not know what you are – and there is only one way to be certain,' He stood up. The Doctor's hearts sank like an innocent woman in an icy pond as he puffed up, called out. 'Guards? Summon the villagers!'

The mud-witches led Yaz, Ryan and Graham out of the woods, up the boggy slope and into Savage Hall.

'All the way through the forest and back where we started,' Ryan whispered, perplexed. They hung back in the hallway, waiting for the witches to reach the top of the staircase, before they dared creep up the creaking treads in stealthy if confused pursuit.

'What would they come here for?' Yaz was baffled, and a bit too noisy.

'Keep your voice down,' Graham hissed, still tracking the berries and now the muddy footprints on the floorboards and leading the way, along the corridor, towards Becka's bedroom door.

'Revenge,' said Graham. 'That's why the undead always come back.'

That made sense. That Becka's victims would come here to confront the woman who killed them, to kill her. What the mud had to do with it, they had no idea, but it explained another element.

'Must be why Becka has that axe,' said Ryan, excited, and then alarmed as they heard the sound of the axe blade dragging along the floor, pulled out of its hiding place.

They found their own hiding place, fast. Sardining into an alcove, as the bedroom door opened and Mother Twiston stood in the frame, grimy teeth flashing in a twisted grin, owning the axe like Scarface with his machine gun, ready to do damage. Soon.

If it was revenge they wanted, they weren't willing to hang around here until Becka came home. Mother Twiston set off, leading them back along the corridor, right by the alcove where Yaz's lungs were about to burst with held breath, then squelched back down the stairs.

They exhaled, but without a chance to feel relieved. Wherever the witches were going with that axe, the gang needed to get there first.

15

The Trials of a Time Lord

The Doctor soon found herself longing for the more laidback timeframe of her last trial. She found it chilling, the efficiency with which the villagers had been rounded up and the ducking stool wiped down and prepped, ready for a second sitting. Almost as chilling as the river looked, grey water rushing on, ready to deliver its deadly verdict.

James stood with the onlookers on the opposite bank, watching, riveted, as Becka's guards marched the Doctor towards the stool to the funereal beat of the drum.

Willa was watching too. She didn't want to but, as with the witness statement, abstaining was not an option. It had hurt her to watch her granny go down, but in a way this was worse. This was her fault, and that righteous indignation she'd felt at the injustice of the world was now replaced by the horrifying knowledge that she was part of it, and this was why the world would never change. Because good people didn't stand up to bad people. They didn't even stand by and do nothing. They were scared, selfish and they joined in, making Yaz's year feel like hell and turning their backs on the Doctor. Willa cursed her weakness and made herself keep watching despite the pain. That would be her punishment.

'I see you brought a gathering, thanks very much,' the Doctor said to Becka, who came to personally supervise putting her into the stool. Becka could trust no one else to do it, now knowing how powerful this witch was, cunning enough to hide in plain sight as the Witchfinder General, when in truth she was the most insidious witch of all. Even now, with judgment nigh, the woman was so immodest, chattering away like an imp.

'Mind if I take off my coat?' The Doctor didn't wait for permission, took it off, surging on. 'Lots in my pockets. Might stop me floating. Course as a woman you don't get to have pockets for a while yet.' She shoved the coat at a guard who took it, nonplussed.

Becka had never seen such a sense of authority, entitlement, in a woman, except for herself. That thought made her shudder. She had to get this over with.

But the Doctor had other plans. Even as Becka backed her towards the stool, the Doctor went on. She wasn't simply playing for time, although she was in no hurry to get ducked; she had a lot more questions that needed answers. Or rather, confirmation. Being tied up had at least given the Doctor the breather she needed to think and some disparate thoughts were starting to fit together.

'A girl called Izzy Flint bullied my friend Yaz so no one would pick on Izzy. That's what you're doing. Pointing the finger at other people so no one points it at you. But what I don't know is – why? What are you hiding, Becka?'

Becka's face gave nothing away. Which in itself gave away so much, of her ability to hold back and not betray her true emotions. Or any emotions, other than contempt.

'Sit down!' she snapped. 'Or would you prefer a hanging?'

Becka pushed the Doctor down onto the cradle of the ducking stool and began to lash her in place with the chains, threatening her up close so the guards couldn't hear.

'Do you know why the ducking stool was invented, Doctor? To silence foolish women who talk too much.'

'Yeah, I did know that and it's daft, because talking's great – like if you talk to me now, I can help.' The Doctor tried to get through Becka's defences, one last time, grasping at the theory that her adversary might be like her. Even with her worst qualities in any incarnation, she would surely still want to talk? So the Doctor kept pushing. 'You've ducked thirty-six people already, and whatever it is has only got worse, hasn't it?'

Becka fumbled – her fingers were less well-trained than her face at giving nothing away – and she dropped the iron chain. When she went to pick it up, her hand touched the stool and sparks flew. A brief flare of bright green sparks, firework hot. Becka recoiled. The Doctor looked closer, marvelling.

'Whoa! What was that?' She sniffed the wood, which was now back to acting like an innocuous log again, but the panic on Becka's face proved the Doctor hadn't dreamt it. 'It reacted to your touch. Why?'

Becka was shaking – with rage? Pain? Fear?

'I warned you to keep quiet.' Her voice was also shaking. Maybe the Doctor could finally get through to her. But kindness wouldn't work. She had to try Becka's method. Threat.

'Rather I asked Willa?' The Doctor looked across the river, ready to shout.

'Silence! Or I shall duck her too.'

That worked, silencing the Doctor more effectively than any ducking stool. Whatever Willa had done, the Doctor didn't blame her, didn't want anyone else harmed. She turned back to Becka, contrite, no more threats, but daring to ask one more thing.

'Last request, I definitely get a last request.' She was fast, all the better to catch Becka off-guard. 'Lend us your hanky.'

'I haven't got one.' Becka froze.

'There's loads in your room,' the Doctor pushed on. 'And an empty medicine bottle. What were you taking the medicine for, Becka?'

Would she crack? Confess? Understand – this was her last chance too; if the Doctor drowned, no one would be left to help her.

Becka thought it over, and made her choice, leaned in, steelier than ever. Radiating hate, beyond anything the Doctor could ever embody.

'Know this, Doctor, once I have dealt with you, I shall go after all of your friends.'

She knew exactly how to cause maximum pain, fear, and finally shut the Doctor up. Becka smiled, showing that she not only meant her threat, but that she would enjoy enacting it. She nodded to the town crier, to let him know everything was ready. He solemnly rang his hand-bell, bringing the crowd to order. The trial was about to begin.

Yaz, Ryan and Graham hurried through the woods, taking a circuitous route at speed, hoping to get ahead of the mud-witches. All of a sudden, Ryan halted.

'Quiet a sec. Listen.'

The others stopped and heard. The tolling of the bell, somewhere in the distance.

Yaz turned, pinning down the direction. 'That's coming from the river.'

'Someone must be getting ducked,' Graham surmised.

'The Doctor wouldn't let that happen,' said Ryan.

They looked at each other, knowing that Ryan was right, and realising in horror what that meant. Without needing to say a word, it was agreed. They set off running, faster, through the forest.

Mud-witches could wait. The Doctor was in danger.

Becka stood on the wooden platform as the ducking stool was winched out over the river. The Doctor's boots dangled, like a child in a swing. That's how small and vulnerable she looked, up there, out on her own, already shivering in the bitter cold.

Turning back to survey her people, Becka began to preach: 'Satan has made our crops fail, bewitched our animals and brought the sickness. His agent sits before you, the most evil witch in Christendom, and she would call herself the Doctor.'

The villagers jeered and roared, baying for blood. Becka noticed that Willa stayed silent, even though the King was right beside her, as if she couldn't bring herself to rejoice in the Doctor's demise. Then she noticed that James was silent too, eyes fixed on the Doctor, but apparently taking no pleasure from proceedings.

Becka called him to attention: 'We bring her to justice in front of our great majesty, King James. Give the word, sire, and we shall duck the witch and save our souls from Satan, once and for all.'

She revelled in the vitriol, so much more than this morning, like something within her had been unleashed and she no longer had to hold back. She whipped the crowd up to fever pitch, performing for their King.

The Doctor's eyes were pleading with him from across the river.

He spoke: 'Duck the witch.'

It was low, almost inaudible, but enough of a spark to catch fire. The people around him took up the chant and it caught on fast, until the whole frenzied crowd was screaming: 'Duck the witch! Duck the witch! Duck the witch!'

A tear leaked from Becka's eye. Not from sorrow or regret, nor even from the hate rising up in her. This was no ordinary tear. Instead of clear saltwater, it was a thin dark trickle, staining her pale cheek with a streak of mud.

She snuck a hanky from her sleeve and moved to wipe the trickle quickly so that nobody saw, except the Doctor, who clocked it from her ducking stool vantage point and gasped: 'I was right.'

Though that was little comfort, as witnessing the tear could only hasten her fate.

Yaz ran out from the trees, Ryan and Graham sprinting after, pushing their way through the crowd, too late.

Becka roared: 'Duck the witch!'

The guard pulled the lever. The ducking stool dropped. SPLASH!

The Doctor hit the icy water and sank down, down, down.

16

Innocence

'Bring her back up now!' Graham yelled, no pretence, a truly fierce Witchfinder General.

The King seemed in a daze, staring at the water where the Doctor had vanished. The surface churned, a few air bubbles popped, and then ... nothing.

'What have you done?' Ryan shouted.

James looked at Ryan, and seemed awkward. 'You will see the result.'

'I'm the Witchfinder General, I'm giving you an order!' Graham commanded Becka.

'I obey only my King,' she replied, resolute.

Ryan tried pleading instead. 'Please, order her to be raised, sire?'

'She's not a witch,' Yaz implored. 'She's your only hope of getting out of here alive.'

Becka could see James wavering, argued her case, the Devil on his shoulder. 'They are all witches, sire. This is Satan testing us.'

'There's no time for this,' Yaz snapped, exasperated. 'Get her out of there!'

'It has been long enough,' James murmured, as if it was him that was surfacing from some kind of trance.

'No it hasn't, we must be certain!' said Becka.

'Bring her up, sire. Now!' Graham was on the brink of decking the King. But Ryan's gentle hand on James's arm proved more powerful.

'Please, Your Majesty?'

'Raise the stool!' James commanded. 'The trial is over.'

To Becka's frustration, the guard obeyed. The stool rose up out of the water, empty. The chains dangled loose, dripping. Everyone stared, stunned.

'No!' Becka roared, raging.

'Where's she gone? What's happened to her?' Ryan sputtered. Yaz and Willa looked back at him, lost. Graham shook his head, fearing the worst.

The King was stunned, blinking at the stool, baffled. 'Where is she?'

'Looking for me?'

The Doctor emerged from behind the bushes on the opposite bank. Drenched again, but alive and surprisingly chipper.

'Doctor!' Yaz grinned.

'She truly is a powerful witch,' James stared in awe.

'No, sire.' The Doctor grinned at him and called out to address the crowd, who stared, silent, agog. 'I am no witch. I'm just good at holding my breath, and getting out of chains, thanks to a very wet weekend with Houdini – hi team! Gang. Fam. No?'

Yaz, Ryan and Graham looked at each other and laughed, releasing the tension.

Willa was overwhelmed. The words burst out her, with no more care for self-preservation. 'I'm so sorry, Doctor, I was scared.'

The Doctor nodded, understanding, forgiving, and turned to Becka to hammer it home. 'You see? That's all it takes, Becka, start there. Tell me the truth.'

Suddenly Becka realised, the world had shifted and, somehow, she was on trial now. Her platform wasn't the seat of power any more. She was the accused, standing in the dock, and now it was her turn to come clean. But how could she?

She pressed her hanky to her mouth, trying to keep it all in, the truth, and more. Even breathing was hard, as if her lungs were flooding. She heaved a breath and hollered, clinging on to the essence of Becka as long as she could.

'The Doctor survived! She is a witch!'

Becka pointed her finger, but the crowd was no longer entranced. The spell was broken and they fell silent, remembering all the loved ones they had lost.

'For the last time, I am not a witch,' affirmed the Doctor, 'and despite appearances, neither are they.'

Out of the trees, the undead Mother Twiston emerged, axe in hand, leading her four mud-witch handmaidens through the mist. The villagers shrieked, panicked and scattered, running back home and beyond if they could, needing no more proof that Bilehurst was cursed and that even the King couldn't save them.

'We have to get over there.' Ryan turned to James. 'Your Majesty … ?'

'Yes, of course, we must confront those agents of Satan, even in the face of witchery … ' James hadn't moved, perhaps hoping the gang would go without him and he could slope off home.

'Seriously, not witches. Bodies possessed by alien mud! Come on!' Yaz pulled the confounded King along with her and Willa, Graham and Ryan, running for the bridge, trying to get to the other bank before the mud-witches closed in.

'You might wanna come and stand with me now, Becka,' the Doctor said. 'Because they look like they've come for you.'

Becka saw it was true. The mud-witches' black eyes were locked on hers and they licked their drooling lips, agitated, eager. Becka was transfixed, terrified. She hid the hanky up her sleeve and stumbled down off the platform to hide behind the Doctor. No matter how much Becka despised the woman, she would do anything to save herself.

Mother Twiston kept coming, axe blade gleaming, guttural voice intoning: 'I will be with you, in the water, in the fire, in the air—'

Becka couldn't bear it. She screamed: 'Stop! Please stop!'

Then the strangest thing happened. Mother Twiston did stop, and lowered the axe, as if on command. The other mud-witches stopped too. Stopped dead – or undead – a few feet away from the Doctor and Becka.

The Doctor held very still as her gang came closer: Yaz taking care of Willa and Graham close beside James, who now cowered behind Ryan, watching the confrontation unfold.

The Doctor stared from the motionless mud-witches to Becka, who seemed frozen with fear. The trace of the mud tear still marked her cheek. 'They're obeying you. What happened, Becka? I thought they'd come to kill you but they haven't, have they?'

The Doctor looked at the mud-witches with fresh eyes, seeing that their very unfresh eyes were lit not with hunger, but with reverence. They were clawing the air, reaching out to Becka, but not to kill her, or fill her. They didn't need to. Becka had been forced to pull her hanky out again and was coughing into it.

'Of course,' the Doctor breathed. 'They've come to *join* you. It's in you, just as it's in them. And none of you can hide it any more,' said the Doctor.

'In the earth,' Mother Twiston rasped, gazing at Becka in something close to adoration. That worship scared Becka more than anything. It meant that she wouldn't merely be killed. Her worst fears would come true and no one here could save her. Except maybe this Doctor?

'What happened? Tell us, while you still can. Before whatever it is fills you up, entirely.'

The Doctor knew. There was no hiding it any more. Becka had to confess to save her soul.

17

What Lies Beneath

'I cut down her favourite tree.' Becka looked at Mother Twiston. Something in the mud-witch seemed to understand. Which was more than the Doctor did. This was not the confession she'd expected. Becka elucidated, a little. 'It was spoiling my view of the hill.'

As with all family fall-outs, there was a lot more to it than could be spilled out in a crisis-point confrontation. Years of simmering resentments, grudges from childhood nursed to full strength, and personality clashes festering on a genetic level. It had all culminated in a moment of bloody-minded violence that had triggered total devastation, so Becka stayed focused on that moment, not going any deeper. For even she didn't know all the secrets that were buried in Bilehurst Cragg.

Unlike with Willa, Mother Twiston had raised Becka since she was a baby, as if she were her own, and for this Becka could never really forgive her. Because that would mean that Mother Twiston was some kind of saint, and not a bad person like Becka who didn't heal people or worship nature or feel utter contentment gazing out at Pendle Hill changing through the seasons. Becka hated the way they had to live, in that grotty little cottage with its stinking potions and fetid brews. She hated traipsing through the woods to gather fungi, getting her only skirts dirty and wearing holes in her only boots. Most of all she hated tramping up the hill to gather leaves from that rotten, creepy old tree. Whatever made Mother Twiston love it made it repulsive to Becka and she prayed for it to get struck by lightning so they'd never have to go there again.

Becka prayed a lot, partly to defy Mother Twiston, who had little interest in the church, but also because it was the only power Becka had to change her lot when she was young. As she got older, she tried other ways but, being low-born and no particular beauty, she struggled to win the affections of any young men who might be going places. Becka seriously contemplated getting herself to a nunnery, just to get out of Bilehurst and at least have some peace. Once Willa moved into the cottage, life had become even more unbearable, as the noxious runt hung on Mother Twiston's every word and loved nothing better than a yomp in the forest or to climb up the wretched tree and hug it.

Becka had resigned herself to having to marry God to escape this living hell, and waited behind at church one Sunday to find out exactly how a girl like her could join a convent, which is when she met Richard Savage and realised a marriage closer to home could be just as chaste and a lot more profitable. She had seen Richard before of course, he was at church every week, but he had always been a fat old man in the front pew, as distant to her as a portrait of the King. Now he was close enough for Becka to hear him discussing his administrative problems with the priest, and she offered to help. Not out of saintliness like Mother Twiston, but to help herself. To make herself indispensable to this man who would surely die soon after their marriage from being fat or old.

Not soon enough for Becka, but luckily some of her knowledge of fungi proved useful after all and, having got rid of Richard, eventually she was free to assume the role she believed she was born to – Queen of Bilehurst Cragg. With a little judicious revision of her ambitions, Becka had decided that being the biggest fish even in such a stagnant pond was her destiny and she enjoyed the sinful kick she got out of wielding power over people who had dismissed her as unworthy. She even enjoyed the thought of them suffering, losing their crops, their livestock, and even sometimes their lives, from the wretched conditions they lived in while she luxuriated in the splendour of Savage Hall. But she had to tread carefully, appear humble, concerned and holy, praise the Lord from the front pew and preach the doctrine that goodness would be rewarded and the cause of all their troubles was evil that she would root out. Witch-hunt fever was gripped the land and all the villages in the vicinity were taking action. The time had finally come for Becka to step up and take down her targets.

It was while she was planning her first witch-hunt, against prime target Annie Clay, that Becka was looking out of the window at Pendle Hill, pondering a new portrait painting, and her eyes sharpened on the tree. She hadn't been there in years, but the deep loathing in her belly still remained and in that moment the tree came to embody everything she hated about her old life – the way she'd been forced to live all those years when she was clearly meant for better things. If she could have wrenched it out by the roots, she would have, but the roots were so ancient and deep it would have been impossible even for a dozen men, so instead she took an axe and she cut it down herself. Already she had its new purpose in mind for the witch trials but, as she swung the axe, her true motivation flooded through her. Pure hate. Sweet vengeance.

How could she have known what force she would unleash?

The axe hitting the tree released the tendril, some essence of the Morax Queen mixed with the mud that had interred her for millennia. Without Becka's hate, the tendril might have merely reached a few inches into

124

the air and then melted back down, unable to take form. But the instant a few particles of Sselde were freed, they scented Becka's hate and the tendril sharpened, reaching out for this kindred spirit, who happened to have tucked her skirts up all the better to chop the tree down, leaving her legs bare. The tendril sharpened and jabbed, Sselde's essence entering Becka's pores. All Becka felt was a sting, although the brown mark left on her leg didn't look like an insect bite. She rubbed at it briefly, then carried on slamming the axe at the tree trunk, while Sselde's particles entered her bloodstream and settled in, finding their perfect form to inhabit in this new world.

Becka did not know the truth about what happened that day on the hill, any more than she knew the truth about who she really was.

As she'd set about having the tree repurposed into a ducking stool, Becka had no idea that her real mother was not some long lost Twiston sister but was the original witch in the woods, Annie Clay, who gave her baby girl away so that the child wouldn't have to grow up with the stigma Annie had always lived with. Annie wanted to give her daughter a better life in the village, with a good, kind woman who would care for her and keep the secret.

And Mother Twiston had kept the secret, as had Annie Clay, even when her now-grown daughter accused her of being a witch. Annie had long watched

Becka from a distance and been so proud of her achievements. It broke her heart to see her own flesh and blood turn on her, but it also made a terrible sense to Annie, the punishment she deserved for being a bad mother, an end to the pain of loneliness that had been her only constant companion, and hopefully an end to the pain of Bilehurst. On some level, Annie really believed she was a witch, and that if she was gone, the village could thrive.

As Becka lashed her to the stool and prepared to duck her, Annie looked out at the crowd. Becka's father could have been any man in the village, and in a way he was all of them. They had made Becka together and it was fitting that she had risen to lead them. Looking across the water into her daughter's eyes, Annie had to believe Becka was leading them into the light. Annie hung on tight to that hope, and the boundless love inside, as she plunged into the river and everything went dark.

Becka would never know that the woman she judged to be the cause of all the evil in Bilehurst was her mother, the closest person to herself in the world. And if she had known, it wouldn't have saved Annie, only given Becka more reason to shut Annie up and get rid of her. Perhaps Annie had known that. Mother Twiston certainly had, keeping her promise to Annie even after she'd buried her. However zealous the witch-hunts became, Mother Twiston never thought Becka would risk accusing her own family, for fear of guilt by association, so she continued to play mother even as Becka's actions appalled her. Until she understood the reason for them.

When more than thirty women had died by the ducking stool and nothing was better, Becka called Mother Twiston to Savage Hall, brought her up to the bedroom after dark and confided in her, as the closest thing she had to a mother and doctor.

'Something lay beneath the tree. When I cut it down, I awoke hell. Satan himself attacked me, poisoned me.' Becka's ghost-pale face flushed with shame.

She peeled up the skirt of her nightdress to show her bare shin where a dark mark festered. A witch's mark, some would have said, but Mother Twiston did not believe in such things. She looked closer. It was a black suppurating wound, under the skin like a bruise but oozing through a pinprick in the centre where the infection had entered, and spreading around its edges, darkening the veins beyond.

'I felt it growing inside me. The mark of Satan. I tried to scrub it out. I fought it. I took medicine. I prayed. But it grew. I did God's work in the hope that it would save me.' Becka looked up, desperate.

Mother Twiston found it hard not to soften, instinctively wanting to help any suffering creature, even one who had brought it on herself. She shook her head at the misguided child and stayed as practical as she could manage, in triage mode: 'It's not the mark of Satan, there is no such thing and praying won't save you, nor will killing more poor women. What medicine did you take?'

'Your special medicine. I got Tessie the maid to procure it for me, so you wouldn't know it was for me. I think it helped a little, slowed the spread for a while, but Tessie said the medicine ran out.'

'It was made from the special tree, so I cannot make more.'

Those resentments rushing between them like the icy river. Mother Twiston's upset and disappointment. Becka's shame and indignation. They all had to stay buried so they could deal with the more tangible problem at hand.

'Is there anything else you can do to cure me?' Becka asked.

Mother Twiston shook her head again, but not with judgment now, with true sorrow. 'I do not believe in Satan, but whatever this is, it is not natural. There is nothing I can do.'

'Yes, there is.' Becka had held out little hope for a miracle medicinal cure. She revealed the real reason she had brought Mother Twiston here. She reached under her bed, and brought out the axe, held it out.

Mother Twiston stared in horror, refusing to believe what she was being asked to do, until Becka spelled it out.

'Cut it out of me. I have tried, but I cannot do it myself. Cut it off and seal the wound with the fire. I will bite on the pillow so no one will hear. We can say that I fell, broke my leg. You had to cut it off to save me. I need you to save me, please, Mother?'

It was so long since Becka had called her that, the rush of emotion almost clouded all the wrongs Mother Twiston had witnessed. She wanted to save her. She took hold of the axe, raised it, but she couldn't do it. She couldn't inflict harm like this even to save, even if it would save, which she doubted. If anything, she feared it would make Becka worse, increasing her pain and rage and giving her a reason to turn on her and Willa. Mother Twiston put the axe down, and shook her head once more, with regret.

'I am sorry, my child. If it helps you to pray, then you should pray for this sickness to kill you swiftly and painlessly without infecting anyone else. And you should pray for forgiveness. No one needs to believe in God or the Devil to know that you have done wrong, my love. So much wrong.'

Becka wept, ashamed and afraid. Mother Twiston wept too as she held Becka, hoped she had got through to her and that the witch-hunts would stop. But deep down, she feared, she would be next.

No, Becka couldn't tell the Doctor, King James or anyone else of this, except for the two moments with

129

the axe – first her churlish attack on the tree, and then Mother Twiston's failure to cut the infection out. This was the abridged version that made sense to her – an evil unleashed from the demonic hill that forced its way into her and needed fighting with the Lord's light, and finally with an iron blade, just to be certain.

'I needed her help.' Becka poured her heart out as much as she could, as much as she knew, letting them see her fear. 'I begged for it, to lance this evil out of me. But she was too weak.'

She struggled to win any pity. The Doctor and her crew were a tough crowd.

'So you killed her by ducking?' asked the Doctor, terse.

'I had to. She knew!' Becka coughed gobbets of filth into her hanky. It was all coming out now.

'You killed people to try and save yourself.'

But now something was surging inside of her, calling time on mortal preoccupations. Becka had no more time for this pointless trial. 'I can't fight it any more, Doctor.' She staggered away from her surly accuser, going to join the beckoning mud-witches.

Seeing the culprit reach a safer distance, James regained a rush of bravery, coming out from behind Ryan to deliver his royal judgment: 'You cannot fight it because you are the witch!'

Becka welcomed the verdict, grateful, relieved. 'I have let Satan in. I have failed you, sire.' She smiled; it felt so much better to own it, to let it take hold of her at last. 'I *am* the witch!'

18

Kill Them All

The Doctor could see Becka was lost, which made her more worried about everyone else. 'Whatever's going on inside of her, this isn't going to be pretty. Get behind me.'

As Willa, James and the gang gathered behind the Doctor for protection, Mother Twiston and her witches crowded in on Becka, her own fam, coming to protect her.

'What's happening to her?' Yaz asked.

'I dunno,' said Graham, troubled, 'but it puts me in mind of when you're on the beach and your mum and dad stand around you with towels so's you can get changed.'

'Changed into what, though?' Ryan was pretty sure it wouldn't be swimming trunks.

Becka's legs gave way and she sank down, skirts billowing up, like a broken doll dropped on the muddy bank. The rancid handmaidens surrounded her, twisting and snarling, warding the others off. Becka searched through their defensive wall, looking for the Doctor. Her eyes streamed with tears, some still human, salt water thinning the black mud. Her voice still trembling, terrified for her soul.

'I tried to hold Satan back. I'm so scared. Please forgive me?' Finally Becka took Mother Twiston's advice and begged for mercy, but had she left it too late?

Before the Doctor could speak, Becka threw her head back and let out an inhuman roar, ridding this body of the woman who wanted forgiveness and filling it with another who wanted the opposite – revenge.

First her fingernails turned, dirt gathering in the tips as if she just needed a good scrub, but no scrubbing would get rid of this muck. It seeped out through the cuticles and suddenly her fingers and hands were filling up with mud from inside. It pulsed through her veins, discoloured her skin and coated it with a thick filthy carapace. Last of all it flooded up her chest, neck, throat and through all the capillaries of her face, replacing any softness with a feculent rind and slicking over her eyeballs. Mud seeped out through the roots of her hair, coating it. Her head seemed to be moulded from the wet earth, a beautiful, monstrous mud sculpture, throbbing with life.

The mud-witches howled, glorying in Becka's transformation.

'She is possessed by Satan!' James gasped.

'Not by Satan. By something not of this Earth,' said the Doctor, bracing herself for the answers she'd been seeking, as everything that had festered under the surface of Bilehurst Cragg was unleashed in its landowner. Whatever was in the land had taken her over and was ready to reveal itself.

'Morax,' the creature snarled, ending all doubt. 'I am Sselde, the Morax Queen.' Becka may have feigned a lack of self-doubt, but this new iteration was the real deal, the embodiment of pure self-belief. Her voice was deep, harsh and unequivocal, no trace of any question or tremble in it.

The Morax Queen rose up. Not in her true form; that was lost forever. But this new form suited her better than the one she'd had to endure for the last few millennia. She looked like Becka, but infinitely stronger, oozing mud, exuding power, and on a mission. She had had so long to plan and now finally it was happening.

'Hand me your king!' Sselde commanded.

'What?' James yelped, scurrying back behind Ryan.

The Doctor stepped forward, gratified that the alien was talking now, making sense. She could work with that. She accepted that they might not automatically make friends, but at least she could size up the scale of the threat.

'Haven't you got your own king, or is he hiding?'

'He does not hide,' Sselde spat, insulted by this upstart's suggestion. 'He waits. We have all waited for too long. Trapped in the hill.'

'Pendle Hill?' The Doctor glanced up at the huge hulk looming over them, omnipresent, yet it had never once occurred to her that it might be at the root of all the mysteries. Perhaps naively, she'd assumed it was just a hill, albeit with some spooky mythology. Not some kind of alien base.

'Our prison.' The Queen also threw a glance at the hill, but hers was hate-filled. 'The mighty Morax Army. Captured and imprisoned on this pitiful planet for war crimes.'

'Pendle Hill is a prison for an alien army,' the Doctor said, reframing everything.

'Oh well, it's obvious when you put it like that!' Graham boggled, thinking back to his walking tour. And there was him, worried about spraining his ankle on a fox hole or getting his crown jewels pranged when Grace made him clamber over a barbed wire fence. If only they'd known the real danger was a murderous legion of mud aliens!

'Imprisoned no more. The lock was broken,' the Queen crowed.

'What lock? How was it broken?' The Doctor gobbled up each new piece of intel. This Morax was giving her a feast after Becka had forced her to fast all day. It was great in a way, getting to the bottom of it. But it was bound to have a catch. The cocky ones were forthcoming, but they were always trouble.

Sselde didn't care to respond on the Doctor's terms. She had a mission to fulfil. She raised her hands and roared: 'Now the Morax Army shall rise again and take form. Your king shall be filled with our king. And we shall be free to fill all of you. To fill this whole planet with rage and force and hate and Morax!'

The mud-witches raised their arms in sync with their Queen and together they sent out a blastwave, knocking the Doctor off her feet. Knocking everyone to the ground. Except for James.

He stood, frozen in terror, as his protectors lay at his feet like Alfonso, lost, leaving the Morax Queen smiling voraciously and the mud-witches coming towards him.

19

In the Fire

Night was falling as the Doctor blinked and emerged from the blackness. As soon as her eyes came into focus on the inky hill, it all came back to her, with a flood of new revelations. Her body might have been unconscious, but her mind had used the time like a smartphone downloading a new update. While she'd lain inert, it had worked to piece all the parts of the puzzle together, so that she'd be ready when she came around. Brains were funny that way. Sometimes the best thing for a breakthrough was having a good kip. It was easier to embrace the mad logic of reality through a dream.

The Doctor sat up sharply, with total clarity, knowing exactly what she had to do now. Was this how it was for the Morax Queen, she wondered? All those years, trapped, dreaming inside of that hill, and now nothing could hold her back?

Well, they'd have to see about that.

She jumped up and set to, waking up Yaz, Ryan, Willa, and Graham, who all swam back to consciousness a bit blearier, especially Graham who had banged his head in the fall and could have done serious damage if it wasn't for the excellent quality of the hat.

'Come on, Witchfinder, up you get.' Yaz pulled Graham to his feet.

He looked around, disoriented, baffled. 'What's happened to His Majesty?'

'They took him.' The Doctor filled him in, her words tumbling out. 'Luckily for us. Otherwise they'd have killed us with the blastwave, but they needed James to be in good nick, couldn't risk damaging him, so they had to use a less lethal setting on us. Still, it was quite a blast, wasn't it? Haven't had a hangover like this since the Milk Wars of Keston 5.'

She busied herself, scrambling down to the ducking stool and working the levers to guide it back to the bank.

'What are you doing with that?' Ryan asked.

The Doctor grinned. This was the good bit. The bit where she could feel nicely triumphant before having to actually face the alien foe. 'Tell them, Willa, what Bilehurst means?'

Willa frowned. 'It means sacred tree on a hill.'

'Thought it must – knew about the hill bit, and the tree bit, but not the sacred bit. Hadn't made the connection, until I realised – it's all connected. The prison in the hill. The lock. The tree Becka chopped down out of spite. The tree this ducking stool is made from. The tree that isn't a tree …' Her eyes glittered as she sonicked the tree trunk that the stool was fashioned from, revealing its inner workings to her frowning audience: not wood at all, but complex, glowing circuitry like fairy-lights twinkling with eerie hieroglyphics.

'It's ancient alien technology,' the Doctor enthused, awed. 'Beautiful and broken. A very old, very advanced, bio-mech security system. A lock, to keep the Morax Army imprisoned. That spark I saw – it responded to Becka's touch because of the Morax infection inside her.'

Ryan still seemed fuggy and unsure. 'Hang on, just run this by me again – so Pendle Hill's a prison?'

The Doctor nodded, sonicking every inch of the ducking stool, adjusting the screwdriver to comprehend as much of the circuitry as was possible. It wasn't easy, given the obscurity of the system, but she strove to find the fundamental building blocks and iterated from those with a dash of nous and a good dose of hunch, like decoding the Rosetta Stone on fast forward, and elucidating on fast forward as she worked.

'From what Becka said, the Morax are royals, with soldiers, pretty brutal ones at that, exiled for war crimes, scrambled down into their primal form.'

Yaz cut in: 'And they stay in prison until Becka Savage goes at that tree?'

'It can't be much of a lock if she can break it,' Graham scoffed, with the air of a tradesman tutting at substandard work.

'It's old,' argued the Doctor. 'Probably from before this planet was even inhabited. The ones who made it are long gone. There's been no one around to oil it so it's eroded over billions of years.'

'My granny tended to it,' said Willa. 'She worshipped it. Made her special medicine from its leaves.'

Another penny dropped for the Doctor: 'Yes! That's why it worked so well on Becka's infection. Slowed the progression right down, which was good in that it held the Queen back from taking her over. But bad because it gave her chance to kill all those innocent people, thinking it would make God save her. Not knowing the only thing that was keeping her alive was the magic potion from this tree.' The Doctor shook her head. The capacity of humans to work directly against their own best interests never ceased to astonish her.

'But not all the Morax got out?' said Ryan, cottoning on. 'She said there was an army?'

'Only an advance party seems to have escaped so far. The Queen who first infected Becka, and then a few others who've taken time to work their way down the hill. Maybe they got into the livestock en route, which is why she thought the horses had Satan in them, why they got shot. But she couldn't contain a dispersed threat like that, moving through the earth, so eventually it made it all the way through the woods and into the graveyard. The tree stump and its roots are still in place, keeping the King and the rest of the Army in the hill. But now Queenie's got that axe, it won't be long before Pendle Hill spews out a tidal wave of Morax soldiers, enough to fill every body on Earth, living and dead, and then restart their wars across the universe. From the cut of her jib, she's spent her time on revenge rather than rehab.'

'Right so, she's got an invincible alien army, we've got what? Nothing!' Graham shook his head. 'How can we stop her?'

The Doctor grinned at him. 'According to my calculations, this ancient alien wood should be like Semtex to the Morax. That's why it made such a good lock. So come on, help me break it up.' She kicked at one of the branches snaking off the stool, snapping it with her boot.

'Break it up?' Yaz frowned. She'd kept up really well until now. 'Why? What for?'

The Doctor glanced up at the last fingers of sunlight, losing their grip on the hill. 'No time for that right now. Just help me smash it, quick!'

A fire blazed in the pit where Mother Twiston's cauldron once hung, a tiny pool of warm light in the darkness that cloaked the village. The Doctor stood close to the fire, but not to dry herself off this time. She'd barely noticed her clothes were still soaking. Nothing like an encounter with a genocidal alien queen to take your mind off laundry. She was using the flames for their light as she sonicked a chunk of the smashed-up tree, around the size of a Rubik's Cube and a sight more fiendish, but she was sure it was the right piece. Well, fairly sure. Certainly keeping everything crossed that it was.

Yaz, Graham and Ryan also held pieces of the broken stool, branches snapped into substantial torches, which they held in the fire until the alien wood caught light, flames giving off a white-green glow.

'Anti-Morax weaponry.' The Doctor wasn't grinning now. Weaponry was never her first choice, but this was defensive and essential to her plan. 'The smoke should be toxic to Morax. That should be enough to fend them off so that you can rescue King James and I can get to the tree.'

She was surprised that no one noticed the number of shoulds and cans in that plan, as opposed to any definitely wills. It was both pleasing and scary how they trusted her.

'Then what happens?' asked Ryan, watching the trails from his torch marking the air like a sparkler.

'Then I fix the lock, putting all the Morax energy back in the slammer.'

Ryan and the others nodded approval. It helped the Doctor believe that it might just work. *Might.*

'One more thing, Doc.' Graham took off his hat and put it on the Doctor's head instead, dubbing her: 'Morax-finder General, back in command.'

Ryan and Yaz beamed. The Doctor didn't know if it was them or the hat, but wearing it helped a lot. If you had to take on the might of the Morax, best to do it with these guys, and in great millinery.

'It's a very flat team structure.' She smiled at Graham, grateful. 'Ready for battle?'

'Yes, we are.' Willa approached with an unlit torch. They'd told her to wait in the safety of her cottage until they came back, but Willa had rebelled. She had given up ceding power to authority, even the Doctor. However frightening the prospect, she knew she had to do the right thing and go with her gut. She thrust her torch into the flames.

'You don't have to, Willa,' Yaz watched her, impressed, but worried that Willa had been through enough today, and ever since the witch-hunts began.

'It's time to stop being scared,' Willa replied.

Yaz nodded, proud.

'Little bit of scared is no bad thing,' cautioned the Doctor. 'The Morax are way more dangerous than Becka ever was.'

Willa had her answer ready. 'Only I know the path up the hill, so you need me to lead the way.' Her torch took flame, and a new light fired in her eyes, scorching the grief and fear. 'There are more powerful people here than kings and queens. There's us. Together.'

The Doctor was fired up. No more mights, maybes and and finger crossings. This would work. It had to. She nodded to the girl, the smallest of them all. 'Lead on, Willa Twiston.'

Willa did, and they all followed, a tiny line of green flames, dwarfed by the hill and by the task facing them, but undaunted. Onwards and upwards they climbed, to save the King, and the world, and many worlds beyond.

20

Exit the King

Starless night on Pendle Hill, a lonely stretch of storm-battered bracken and bog with nothing to protect it from the elements now the great tree had gone. The wind whipped across the heath, black clouds shrouded the moon and the mist hung low, swirling in eddies around the ravaged tree stump where the witches gathered. Tree roots snaked down into the earth, trying to hold it in place, but thin tributaries of mud were already trickling out, more fragments of Morax escaping, ahead of the tsunami to come. The mud-witches drooled in thrilled anticipation as their Queen took the axe and commanded their quaking prisoner.

'Kneel before Morax!'

King James looked down at the morass of mud and Morax, really not keen on the idea of kneeling in it, let alone the horrors beyond. To his surprise, instead of his own unholy fate, he found himself thinking of his mother, who had also had to kneel before her axe-wielding executioner. He had never let himself really think about that, about how she must have felt, how she must have hoped that God would intervene and save her soul. He prayed that things would be different for him. Because he was special ... wasn't he?

'I said *kneel*, feeble human!' Sselde snarled, and the witches pushed him down. His knees sank inches deep in the mire and his head was shoved into the splintered cleft on top of the stump. He could see the Queen at the other side, lining up the axe. He thought of the Doctor, jabbering away, and the image inspired him. If he could find his tongue, perhaps he could find out more, negotiate.

'Tell me what you are, you Satanic creature?'

'You will see. We will rule this world.'

'*We?*' This was what he needed to clarify, because his first thought had been that she'd want to marry him, which was understandable as he was essentially the most important man on Earth, but then he was already married and so was she by the sounds of it, and though he wasn't averse to a discreet indulgence here and there, he really drew the line at fraternising with the likes of this demonic harpy.

It was safe to say that James really hadn't grasped the finer details of Sselde's masterplan. But he was about to.

'Your body will be filled with my Morax King.' The Queen had no more inclination to discuss matters with James. He was merely a vessel to her. A royal vessel, which was perfect for her purposes, but if James hadn't come to Pendle, she'd have made do with whatever high-ranking man she pleased. Proximity was the most important thing for swiftness. She couldn't wait any longer. 'Come to me, my love!'

James stared, helpless, the reality of what was about to happen seeping into his mind like the mud seeping through his beautiful garter. He no longer prayed to be saved, but for a quick, merciful death like his mother's. Even beheading was preferable to this vision of a Morax-infused James and Becka, covering the world with their filth.

Sselde swung the axe back and brought it slamming down, jagging into the stump so close to James's face it trimmed his whiskers. His relief that it left his nose intact didn't last long. The stump began to rumble, a low, groaning, gushing sound from deep down in the belly of the hill. Small bubbles of mud appeared where the blade had sliced, then as the rumble grew louder, closer, faster, the axe flew out and the stump erupted.

'Satan rises!' James yelped. He had no other words to process this, no way to comprehend the gigantic tendril shooting up into the sky … but not showering down. It stayed upright, in one piece, because it was one thing. The Morax King.

The end of the tendril formed the grotesque features of a half-remembered face that looked down on the doll-like figures below. He searched their faces with hollow eyes and recognised his Queen in her new

149

form, gazing up at him with love and longing. Then he saw the body of the man she had procured for him. He lashed and roared, eager to pour his essence into those limbs, that skin, and feel again, breathe again, kill again.

James stared up at this devil incarnate that was about to devour him. He tried to pray: 'I may fear you, but I have my faith—'

The Morax King roared again and rushed down at him, its hellmouth opening up like a tunnel in the tendril tip, ready to engulf James.

'Please, Lord, save me!'

'Or alternatively, Witchfinders United, at your service!' the Doctor called out.

Sensing danger, the tendril veered away to see the Doctor and her band of blazing saviours, cresting Pendle and striding towards the stump. Toxic smoke from the green flames blew across the hilltop and sent the tendril reeling back. The witches coughed up gobbets of mud, and the Queen's black eyes smarted as the Witchfinders moved in, wafting the torches, fending them off.

'You'd better back off!' The Doctor came towards the Queen, who grabbed the axe from the ground. 'Let the king go, Morax. You can't have him or this planet.'

'Yeah, get away from him!' Ryan got between James and the King-tendril, fighting the beast off with his torch, getting close enough for the smoke to scorch the raging face, which screamed and recoiled in agony.

James stumbled, slipped over, but Ryan caught hold of him: 'I've got you, sire.'

'My protector,' James whimpered, clinging to him tightly.

Graham, Yaz and Willa wielded their torches at the mud-witches, keeping them at a safe distance from the Doctor, but there were only three of them and four of the creatures. Mother Twiston broke away and came for Willa, ready to fill her and convert her to the Morax cause.

'Watch out for your granny!' Yaz yelled.

Willa swung around to face the Morax, her grief and upset coming out as rage.

'You're not my granny. Let her rest.' She thrust the torch right at the monstrous old woman, who shrank back, hissing. Willa hated to cause pain, but this had to end now.

'Go on, Morax, back into your cell.' The Doctor squared up to the Queen, giving her a choice between a dignified exit, or the alternative.

Sselde laughed: 'Those flames don't scare me, Doctor. Nothing scares me now.'

'I know you're in there, Becka. I know you're scared.' Willa's voice trembled as she made one last attempt to get through to her cousin. 'I will still be with you! In the water, in the fire, in the air, in the earth …'

*

151

The Queen turned to look at the girl. The words stirred something in her – in some ghost of Becka that still haunted this form, who remembered learning this prayer at her granny's knee and believing in it, once upon a time, long ago. Sselde felt something leaking from her eye. Not mud. A human tear. It sickened her. She needed to kill, rebuild her strength. The Queen glared at Willa, hateful face twisted with scorn: 'Nothing of that pathetic woman remains. No fear, only power.'

The King-tendril loved feeling his Queen's strength again. He lashed and came back at Ryan and James. Spurred on, the mud-witches came at Graham and Yaz. Those torches wouldn't last for long.

'We will fill your King and kill you all!' the Queen decreed.

'Afraid not, Morax,' the Doctor shouted. 'I'm here!'

Sselde realised too late: Willa's attempt to connect was heartfelt, but also tactical – a distraction to allow the Doctor to sprint around the stump to exactly the right spot.

The Doctor pulled the wood chunk from her pocket and shoved it into place. It worked as fast as flicking a switch. The stump lit up, green rays crackling through the tendril, disabling it like a taser on full-stun and sucking it back down.

'Everybody back!' the Doctor shouted. 'I've reactivated the prison. Back you go, King of the Morax.'

The laser bolts crackled up to the clouds, splitting them open so that rain poured down, a smart natural sprinkler system to help wash the convicts back into captivity.

Sselde watched in fury, heart breaking as the tendril form of her King screamed and shuddered back into the dungeon below. Another blast of energy jolted down through the roots, lighting up the whole of Pendle Hill. The ground shook. The mud around them was screaming.

'Jail re-energised!' the Doctor declared.

'No!' the Queen raged. 'What have you done?'

'Feel that security system kicking back in, sucking every Morax cell back. Back down into Pendle Hill. Back out of the bodies they hijacked.'

All as one, the mud-witches dropped, drained of their life force. Freed from the Morax, they were human again. Mother Twiston lay on the ground, serene as if she'd fallen asleep by her favourite tree.

Willa murmured, moved: 'Have peace.'

The King and the army were imprisoned, but Sselde was stronger, hanging on. Like Becka, she would fight to the end to keep hold of her power.

'I will not go!' She fought the security system, the sheer force of her denial resisting its attempts to suck the Queen's essence out and let Becka back in. 'I will never stop!'

'Yes, you will.' Galvanised, King James snatched Ryan's torch and lunged at the Queen, crying: 'Burn the witch!'

'No, sire, stay away!' The Doctor tried to pull him back, but he slipped her grasp.

James thrust the fiery torch into the heart of the Morax Queen. There was a split second where Sselde realised what was happening. Fear flitted across her face – across Becka's face – before the ancient alien Semtex did its job and detonated. The Queen's body exploded, bursting into a bright green blaze that basted mud and guts far across the hill. But her life force was dead now, and the last pieces of her either ran back into the earth with the rain or hung in the air as a few green sparks that faded like a firework and turned to ash, scattering over a tree stump that looked like any other.

The Queen was gone. All the Morax were.

And the Doctor was drenched again, as well as incandescent. The storm raging above was nothing to the look on her face, as she glared at King James.

'What, woman? She was a witch. She confessed.' The King beamed, so pleased with himself. The fact that he still didn't understand anything incensed the Doctor more than the Morax ever could. At least they knew they were the bad guys here.

'So. You got what you came for?' She could barely look at him. Her mind kept replaying the look on

Becka's face – they could have saved her. She could be here now. She could have changed. Or maybe she couldn't. James stood before her, living proof of that likelihood.

'I have vanquished Satan,' he said, that little boy again, clamouring for approval.

The Doctor pulled off the hat and shoved it at him, spelling it out in single syllables a little boy might learn:

'No more witch-hunts.'

Then she turned and walked away into the driving rain.

21

In the Air

A simple 'Yes, Doctor' would have done it. Or a 'Sorry, Doctor, I've seen the error of my ways and it definitely won't happen again.' Or even 'I'm too thick to really understand, but I know you're smarter so I'll just stick with whatever you say and behave myself.'

Unfortunately, the Doctor reflected, James had eschewed this simple route and persisted with his questioning, after they'd laid the innocent women to rest and headed back through the woods. Dawn light spread across the wide sky over Pendle, diluting the horrors of the night, but enlightenment still eluded James.

'If it is not witchcraft, what is it? And do not merely say *alien mud* or *Morax*. These terms create more mysteries than they solve. Tell me the science of it, Doctor,' James implored, relentlessly. 'How they came to be here. How you come to be here! I want to know the science of *you*.'

There was a part of the Doctor that would have loved to take time out and give the King the skinny, but she couldn't even begin to rush the real Enlightenment. That was still a century or so away and before then James had to live and die with his limited concepts of Heaven and Hell and find some kind of satisfaction that didn't involve mass murder.

'You just have to trust me,' was as much as she'd mutter.

'I do! Of course I do. All of you. I trust you with my life.' James paused, for long enough that she thought she'd made progress. 'But I still need to know your secrets.'

'Don't push it,' she warned him, 'or I won't save you from Guy Fawkes.'

James blinked at her, baffled: 'You didn't save me from Guy Fawkes.'

'Not yet,' she said, perilously close to blowing.

James's bafflement deepened: 'But it's already happened, in the past.'

His mind was still reeling from the idea of sentient mud and intelligent women, so there was no way James was ready to wrap it around the notion of time travel. The Doctor decided it was worth the risk to put the wind up him, so she snapped: 'Look, just because you're a big cheese and it led to bonfires and toffee, doesn't mean it's a fixed point in time. Lots that happens can also unhappen, so – don't push it is all I'm saying.'

She flung him a final, fearsome look that any master necromancer would be proud of, and strode off, leaving him silent at last, and contemplating his place in the universe.

Of course, the Gunpowder Plot was a fixed point and the Doctor had no intention of messing with it … although, as can often come to pass, time itself might have other intentions. But for now, the six small figures made their way through the tangle of trees, each person occupying their own place on the spectrum from dangerous or blissful ignorance to terrifying or awesome knowledge.

Graham caught up with the Doctor, having heard the last of her rant, wondering: 'Could you, Doc? Make things unhappen? I don't mean like with Yaz's granny, so people don't exist. I mean doing good things. So if you really wanted to and if you were really careful, you could go back and stop Becka killing those women, or …' Graham got to the bit of the list that the Doctor knew was inevitable. 'You could stop Grace climbing that crane? Or make it so that I could stop her? Or I could do it instead?'

The Doctor was tired. It didn't happen often in this new body. Despite its size, its energy was often boundless, mentally and physically. Even after the sonic mine, she'd come around in record time, but that was a different, simpler kind of tiredness. This was the old kind, that transcended whatever her current biology might mean in a moment of history. It was a weariness amassed over many aeons and identities that made the very concepts of moment and history a cause to curl up in a dark corner. The weight of her knowledge was crushing sometimes, and right now, absolutely knackering. So many ifs – what ifs and if onlys and if things could be differents. Mud monsters she could fight, but those conditional tenses always slipped from her grasp, a battle that could never end. For Graham, old and tired though he felt after being up all night, this was all brand new. The Doctor looked at him and sighed, tried to explain as kindly, patiently, as she could.

'I'd love to, Graham, I wish that were possible, but once you start, where do you stop stopping things? I can't stop my own thoughts rushing on from one moment to the next, so how can I act like a dam across the whole ocean of time, as if I know where it's all flowing? All I can do is try to be here, now, and see – what's right and wrong and try to help things to be more right. Change people's minds to stop doing the bad things, to start doing the better things. To live and let live, and let history tell its own story. I'm on the outside enough. What I really long for is to be in there with the rest of you, living it.'

Graham listened and understood enough to know that the answer was no. That's where he differed from James, and where a bus driver had the edge on a king –

because he had to listen to what people were saying, not get deafened by what he wanted himself, otherwise his bus route would have always ended up at West Ham. What the Doctor said gutted Graham, but he got it, and he got on with it. He couldn't go back and save Grace, and the Doctor couldn't really be like them, but they could both be here now, walking through the woods as the sun rose, the ferns unfurled and the birds sang.

Graham slowed to take in the moment, and Ryan caught up with him.

'Everything all right?' asked Ryan.

'Yep, thanks,' said Graham.

'Cool,' said Ryan, who noted his new trainers were totally filthy, but that was all right too.

They walked on together, maybe not cool, but much cooler than they used to be. The Doctor was right. You could never quite tell where the flow of time was taking you.

Willa and Yaz walked along behind them, talking about the timeless matters of friends and family, boys and girls, thoughts and feelings. Willa felt strangely happy despite all that had happened, and it intensified as she explained and Yaz understood.

'Yeah, there's all kinds of names for it where I come from, traumatic bonding, gaining closure, facing up to your demons …'

'Demons?' Willa asked quickly.

'No, not those kinds of demons!' Yaz laughed.

Willa laughed too, and then felt a sudden stab of sadness as she realised that this was closure, that her new friends would be going now, and that the Yorkshire they came from wasn't as close as just across the border by Barnoldswick. There was a lot more to it. Willa knew better than James. She wouldn't ask for explanations, but she did ask –

'Do you think I'll ever get to see you again?'

Yaz felt that stab of sadness too. She smiled and told the truth. 'I hope not. Because if we do, it probably means you'll be in trouble, and I don't want that to happen. In my job, I only ever get called out when there's something wrong so I never want it to be one of my mates. I want you to keep bossing it and have a brilliant life, all right?'

Willa smiled, grateful, for the truth and the challenge. 'I'll do my best.'

They caught up with the others, ascending the slope down towards the TARDIS. King James hadn't noticed it, being too busy lobbying others to bug the Doctor for him.

'She still does not speak to me, Ryan. Can you get through to her?'

'Afraid not, sire, this is on you.'

James was on the brink of prostrating himself before the Doctor when he stopped dead, staring at the blue box resplendent in a hazy beam of sunlight.

'What apparition is this?' he exclaimed.

'Just another inexplicable wonder of existence you're not going to be able to tell anyone about,' the Doctor sighed, deigning to throw him a few crumbs, now that she was going. Just so he wouldn't go off in a sulk and do some more damage to spite her.

He was grateful, not quite prostrating, but more respectful than he'd ever been of any other woman. 'Doctor, I understand you are displeased with me, and I owe my life to you. Not one word of any of this shall ever be spoken. And even the name Bilehurst shall be erased from all records.'

'As long as all the villagers make it out alive,' Graham warned, not needing a big hat to make his authority felt.

'What will you do, Willa?' asked Yaz.

Yesterday, Willa had been ready to run away in fear. Today, she felt fearless, free of the pain inside, excited by the prospect of going away from here, exploring. Nothing could be as bad as what she'd been through, and she found that the answer was in her, she didn't even have to think about it. 'Find a new home, take after Granny and be a healer. Be a doctor.'

'I reckon you'll be good at that.' Yaz approved.

So did the Doctor, always happy to see a new doctor in the making, and especially this one. Where James had made her feel her age, people like Willa made her feel youthful, hopeful for the future, whatever her knowledge of history might warn her was going to happen.

'One final command, as your King.' James turned to Ryan. 'Come back to London with me, Ryan. Be my protector.'

Graham and Yaz suppressed a snigger. Even the Doctor forgot her anger enough to be amused by the King's soft spot for Sheffield's No. 1 Nubian Prince.

Ryan was flattered, and mildly tempted, but he figured further adventures with the Doctor would be more fun than life as a seventeenth-century bodyguard, even though the life expectancy was probably in the same ballpark.

'It's a kind offer, sire, but I've got stuff to do.' Ryan took off the charm and pinned it back on the King, charming him. 'I'll keep my eye on you, though, so behave yourself.'

As he headed to the TARDIS, Graham added a final warning: 'Or else we will strike down upon thee with great vengeance and furious anger!'

'Ezekiel!' the King beamed, delighted by the biblical reference.

'Tarantino!' Graham grinned and went inside, with Ryan and Yaz, leaving James baffled, not just by Quentin, but by the three people fitting inside the strange blue box, and the Doctor apparently about to follow them.

'What are you all doing?'

The Doctor thought about ignoring him, but Willa was also eager to know, and if there was one thing the

Doctor struggled to resist, it was an apt pupil. She wouldn't make it easy for them, though. She stood in the doorway, eyes glittering, spinning them a riddle, one last golden thread across time and space.

'A brilliant man once said, "Any sufficiently advanced technology is indistinguishable from magic." We're just about to prove him right.' She nodded and went inside.

James and Willa took a moment, taking in her words, trying to make sense of them. Before they could, the box made a noise, like nothing they'd even heard. The leaves whisked up from the ground, swirling in a sudden breeze, and the blue box disappeared.

'Where did they go?' James looked around, bewildered.

Willa looked around and smiled. She knew the answer.

In the air.

22

No More Witch-Hunts?

'Can I come to London with you, please, sire?' Willa asked, breaking King James's reverie and bringing him back down to earth. He seemed confused, even a little irked.

'Whatever for?'

'Well, if I'm going to learn, then I should learn from the best,' Willa flattered him. 'You could apprentice me to one of your physicians. I'd work hard and earn my keep, and then I could protect you from sickness, and from the Morax too, should they ever come back for you. No one else need ever know how we came to be friends.'

The f-word made James physically recoil. 'They won't come back for me. The Doctor has vanquished them. And the less I have to do with any vestiges of this place, the better. No, it is much safer if you stay well away, as far as possible. Wales perhaps. Or Ireland. Or America!' His eyes lit up. 'Yes – the New World.

That's where you should go, my child. Immediately. No witches or aliens to worry about out there.'

He was already striding away, as if the Atlantic Ocean might open up behind him and leave her out of sight and mind for good. Annoyingly for him, Willa ran to catch up.

'But I know no one in America, sire, and I don't have any money.'

'That is the wonder of America. You go there with nothing and no one and make your family, your fortune. You will fare very well out there, Willa, I wish you all the best. Now, you had better hurry along and retrieve whatever you wish to take from Bilehurst, before I have it burned to the ground.'

'Burned? You can't – you heard what Graham said – Ezekiel!'

'I won't burn the people. They will be recompensed and moved on to somewhere nicer, like Preston. We shall say it's a precaution against a plague. That's not even really a lie, and they'll no doubt be grateful to get away from this hellhole – as should you be. The choice is yours – Preston or Jamestown?'

Willa had stopped to gaze up at Pendle Hill, which had never looked less like a hellhole, illuminated by the morning sun. Suddenly she felt the wrench of leaving this place that was in her blood, without the intervention of mud tendrils. Whether it was from here or from a far-off planet at the dawn of time, Pendle

Hill was part of Willa, her roots ran deep. She wanted to grow and learn, but part of her still didn't want to leave. For a moment, she missed Becka, and wished she were with the Morax, sleeping safe, cradled within the hill, instead of out here dealing with the fears of real life. Growing up.

'Will the recompense be enough to get me to Jamestown, sire … ? Sire?'

James had gone. Vanished, not quite as magically as the blue box, but just as permanently.

Willa ran down the track, certain he wouldn't have dared stray from it, but either he'd hidden or ran much faster, because she never caught sight of James again.

And he must have ridden back to London at speed, because soldiers soon turned up at Bilehurst with eviction orders and blazing torches. The recompense was barely enough for a hovel in Preston, never mind passage to the new world. But the plague cover story worked a treat, and the people of Bilehurst took the money and ran. Only Willa hung back long enough to watch the thatched roofs blazing and the splendour of Savage Hall turn to blackened rubble. She wiped the last of her tears, took her money and roamed.

She never got as far as London, but she did learn a little about what happened to James. His witch-hunts did stop, true to his word, and he gradually let it be known that he was rethinking his position on the whole matter of witchcraft, and became interested in rooting out the more tangible evils of tobacco. He held fast to his resolve until the last – almost. On his deathbed, delirious and glimpsing the abyss, he found himself hoping there was some kind of magic that might save him and urged his servants to perform a ritual involving a piglet dressed up as a baby and a half-remembered occult incantation. It didn't work. In his last moments, he called for the Doctor to come and save him again. That didn't work for him either.

And why should the Doctor come and save James? He'd lived well, had a full life and left more of a legacy than most. Whereas Willa Twiston had struggled to carve out her place in the world and fulfil her potential, before she was cut down too soon.

Willa was thirty-eight when the Pendle witch-hunts began again, in 1634, in the turbulent reign of King James's ill-fated son, Charles I. Willa had roamed the North, learned to read and write and to make a modest living from her medical skills. No one would dignify her with the title 'Doctor', but she was well known in the hamlets of East Lancashire as a nurse who knew a lot more than many physicians and charged a lot less. This made many people well, but it also made a few disgruntled physicians peeved enough to spread rumours about Willa's 'unnatural methods and unnatural life' – an itinerant woman who stayed alone in rented rooms and spent every night reading or looking out at the heavens as if waiting for an angel or something darker to descend.

Those rumours caught light when a young man who she tended to in his sickbed accused her of bewitching him. That he was in the grip of a fever didn't seem to devalue his evidence. Nor did the fact that she had to fight him off when he tried to kiss her. All that mattered was his claim that she conjured a black cat and a cloven-hoofed man to subdue him. It was so foolish that Willa wanted to laugh, but she knew the razor-edge of rumours too well and so she fled. To the worst place a suspected witch could go. Home, to Pendle Hill.

Bilehurst was gone. The burning had had a rejuvenating effect on the landscape and lush woodland now covered all traces of the obliterated village. The ashes of Savage Hall had blown away in the gales that whipped across the hillside, and the foundations had sunk under the black bog and bulrushes. Even the witches' graveyard had been reclaimed by nature. No one had any business going back there now and, with witch-hunts on the rise, it would be suicide for a suspect to be found heading up Pendle Hill alone at night. But Willa had no choice. Nowhere else to run. She had to summon the Doctor somehow, even if it meant unleashing the Morax again and risking the future of the planet to save her own life. Because her life mattered, didn't it? Yaz had said that it was meant to be brilliant, but it wasn't. It was over, unless they came when she called.

Willa's feet still knew the path up Pendle Hill. She carried a single flaming torch, lighting the way to where the huge tree stump stood firm, still apparently doing its job. In Willa's other hand, she carried an axe. She wore stolen trousers, tucked in her boots, some kind of defence for when the tendrils spilled out, but not much. The Doctor would have to come fast. Yaz would have to hear her call. Graham and Ryan had to hurry. And if they didn't, what's the worst that could happen? Willa would be filled by the Morax Queen and rule the world, make all these idiots her mud minions. It wasn't what she wanted, but that was on the Doctor. Willa raised the axe up and brought it down –

The blade bounced off the wood, not even leaving a blemish. The stump was no longer like wood, more like solid rock. It wouldn't burn either, when she put the torch to it. It was impenetrable. The security system had learned. It wouldn't be broken again.

Willa broke down, weeping in frustration, looking up at the heavens that had blanked her all these years and crying out for them to listen and take pity and save her.

The only ones who heard were those coming to arrest her, for frolicking with Satan on Pendle Hill, in trousers! Willa's weeping turned to laughter at their pompous piety, and her cackle echoed all the way to Lancaster Castle, where she was locked up in gaol to await death by hanging. Her laughter died. She had given up hope, until she managed to steal a pen and papers from the clerk of the court at the end of her trial.

Willa didn't really believe writing to the Doctor would change her fate, but just putting the words on paper, telling her story, was a kind of hope. One last golden thread to spin, even if it was about to snap like her neck in the noose.

While it lasted, the story felt as though the ending might possibly change. As though she wasn't really in gaol, but was in the woods, the village, by the river, up the hill, all these places in the past, conjured up again and more real to her than the rusted bars on the window or the stinking toilet in the corner.

But when the ending came, it was real and unchangeable.

The papers lay hidden behind the bricks in the wall, and now she was walking, through the bitter morning air and the hateful crowd, towards the hooded hangman. The noose hung, waiting, not a simile. A length of rope knotted in such a way to kill her. After all these years, she suddenly understood exactly how Granny must have felt, looking down into the water, hopeless. No one would still be with her, in the water, in the fire, in the air, in the earth. The universe was cruel and we are all alone in the end.

We. Damn it! Willa couldn't break the habit of hoping, even as the hangman put the noose around her neck. Willa's laugh came back as she mocked her own stupidity. Would she never learn?

The hangman looked at her, curious. Inside the hood, Willa glimpsed – gasped –

The hangman – the Doctor – shushed her, and pulled the lever.

The trapdoor gave way. The noose unravelled from over the top bar of the gibbet. It was knotted in such a way not to kill her, but to let Willa fall safely, down, down –

And be caught by Yaz, Ryan and Graham, waiting under the wooden platform. They broke her fall and carried her rapidly back, out of the way, so the Doctor could jump down through the trapdoor, dying to know –

'What were you laughing at?'

'Nothing. Everything. It is so good to see you, Doctor.'

'You too, Ms Twiston. Cheers for the letter.' The Doctor pulled a fistful of papers from her pocket. The same papers Willa had just hidden in the prison, but much older, centuries-old yellowed parchment. 'Sorry I didn't have time to write back.'

The Doctor grinned at Willa, then swiftly got serious as angry guards overcame their surprise and barrelled in. She grabbed Willa's hand, Yaz grabbed the other, and they all bolted for the TARDIS, slammed the door and warped out of there.

As Willa gazed around at the peculiar, cavernous room, the Doctor apologised, breathlessly: 'Sorry it's all so last minute. We had to wait until you'd finished writing, otherwise we'd never have been able to come back at exactly the right – never mind all that, anyway, the main thing is – we're here now.'

'Where now?'

'Good question, Willa! Or *where when?* Let's see how your story really ends …'

23

I Will Still Be with You

There are so many reasons why I shouldn't be here, at the end of all things. A girl like me, whence I came, should not even be holding a pen, let alone holding the threads that weave the universe together.

And yet it couldn't have ended any other way, as it turns out. The Doctor read my letter in the future. She could still have left me to hang, so as not to interfere with history, but then Yaz suggested she double-check the data in the sonic from when she scanned me, using the more sensitive systems inside the TARDIS. That's when they discovered that I was a bit magic after all.

Granny had raised me on recipes from the tree and it was in my blood, my bones. Something ancient and eternal, which made me different, so I would never really have fitted in. That was enough to justify the Doctor swooping in to save me, and to use the data to take me home, somewhere I might finally and for the first time belong. Where the tree came from, that isn't a tree. A whole not-forest, strung with not-fairy-lights.

So here I am, in this place at the end of time, which has been here since the start of time, where the voices came from that passed judgment on the Morax and seeded some sense of justice in the universe. Those voices are long gone, but there are other voices here.

If I use the threads properly, I can hear all the voices that have ever lived, and I can share them, like I've shared them with you. It's less like a loom than like the biggest network in the universe, and I can use them to tell stories. Tuning in to different lives – not to change them, that is best left to the Doctor – but to help her make things better. To understand, through others, who we are.

We ...

There are three of us here. The three witches, I call us. Me calls us norns. Clara says we're fates. They both call me Mother, because I look older than them, so Mother Twiston is still with us, in a way. But really we are just three girls from the North who have been lucky enough to travel with the Doctor and wound up here, tangled together, sharing our stories, having a laugh, and warming ourselves by the light of the threads, which are golden like her hair.

Like hope.